THE FRIENDSHIP CUP:
PALESTINE TO IRELAND

THE FRIENDSHIP CUP: PALESTINE TO IRELAND

BY
WINNIE CLARKE

MERCIER PRESS

Mercier Press, Cork
www.mercierpress.ie

ISBN: 9781781178089
eISBN: 9781781178812
Audio ISBN: 9781917453547

Table of Contents

Chapter 1.   The Arrival – August 2023   7

Chapter 2.   The First Day   12

Chapter 3.   Tears, Murder, and a Secret   21

Chapter 4.   Second Night   39

Chapter 5.   First Match Day   44

Chapter 6.   Dublin Trip   52

Chapter 7.   Panic Sets In: Only 3 Days Left   63

Chapter 8.   The Real Magic and Another Secret!   70

Chapter 9.   Bundoran Blitz   78

Chapter 10.   Last Day and Good-bye   95

Chapter 11.   The last week before school   103

Chapter 12.   School Starts   107

Chapter 13.   The Aftermath   115

Chapter 14.   One Week After   126

Chapter 15.   Third Week in October   130

Chapter 16.   Marching in Dublin   135

Chapter 17.   No News Is Good News   148

Chapter 18.   The Unbelievable Happens   161

Chapter 1

The Arrival – August 2023

Liam and Sinead were standing at the arrivals area in Dublin airport, looking this way, then that way, and hopping from one leg to the other. They each wanted to get the first glimpse of their visitors. Their mom, Mary, was amused by their enthusiasm. All the expensive camps, games, foreign holidays – and here they were, more excited about hosting a boy for a week. She smiled. Sometimes it was the simple things. But *this* had been anything *but* simple. This had been 2 years in the making, and just yesterday it was still doubtful if the trip was going to go ahead.

The kids had made a sign – Welcome Ali – with a football underneath. Ali was travelling with 14 other boys to play football. Each of them was staying with a host family from Liam's football team. Liam's teammates were also standing around with their own homemade signs.

Eventually, a bunch of very tired-looking boys emerged from the automatic doors. They were accompanied by their 2 coaches. The boys looked so tired and much younger than their 13 years, but each and every one had a big, big smile. Obviously, they were just as excited as the Irish kids!

Quick introductions were made. Itineraries and phone numbers given out, and once everyone was paired with their host family, the 15 boys said good-bye to each other. It would only be for a few hours. Dinner was planned for everyone later that evening at the clubhouse. Ali followed the Murphys to their car. He was walking between Sinead and Liam, who were both talking at once.

Mary interjected, 'Okay, you need to talk one at a time, and slow down. Also, let's say hello in—'

Before Mary could finish, both kids yelled, 'Assalaam 'alaikum.'

Their practice must have paid off, because Ali answered, 'Wa 'alaikum assalaam,' which they understood. But then he kept speaking.

Sinead and Liam smiled, but when Ali continued, Liam started shaking his head. 'No, no, we don't really understand Arabic. We've just started learning,' he said. This time, he spoke s-l-o-w-l-y and clearly.

Ali nodded, and said that he, too, was only just learning English, so he understood. Clearly, his English lessons were going much better than their Arabic lessons.

The Murphy home was in Ballyduff, Co. Leitrim, 2.5 hours away. They stopped halfway for food and toilets. The kids chatted in the back seat for a bit, but they slept most of the journey. Sinead and Liam had been up at 6 in the morning to get to the airport on time, and no doubt Ali, who had travelled all night, was exhausted. And yesterday! Yesterday must have brought a lot of stress to the boys with that last-minute change of travel plans. The whole trip didn't even seem certain, or so the Ballyduffers had been told.

Finally, they were pulling up into the driveway. Gerry, the kids' father, came out to welcome their new guest, with Blacky and Maisie running behind him. The two dogs ran past Sinead, past Liam, past Mary and didn't stop until they came to Ali, who knelt down to pet them. He was laughing and hugging the dogs.

'Well, that's my first question answered. Are you okay around dogs? Obviously, you're a natural, and if our Maisie likes you, well that's high praise, so it is. Isn't that right, kids?' Gerry was pleased.

Everyone agreed. Ali finally detached himself from the dogs' embrace, and they all made their way into the house. Sinead and Liam were being very solicitous, allowing Ali to walk ahead of them and using sign language to point the way. There was only one way to go, so it wasn't entirely necessary, but Ali seemed grateful.

Chapter 2

The First Day

The kids wanted to show Ali their toys, their tree house, their rooms – everything. And Liam was really keen to show him his goal posts and get the football out, but

Mary insisted on having tea first. Tea was a ritual in the Murphy house. Whoever arrived always had to have the obligatory 'cuppa', and be warned, if you don't like tea, just accept it anyway from Mary Murphy. There was always something tasty to accompany the tea.

Tea drunk, the kids ran outside. The village was nearby, and the whole village met at the field. Soccer, Gaelic Football, tig – you name it – the field had it all covered. It was like their watches were all synched: the village children arrived with the visiting boys at just the same time. Soon, some boys and girls were playing football and some tig. Others watched while texting and chatting. Ali told Liam he was tired and didn't want to play football. Sinead happily kept him company and introduced him to many of the local children. Every other boy on Ali's team was glad to play.

The visiting boys were small – even the children seemed to notice this now – but boy, did they know how to play footy. Liam whispered to his friend Danny, 'They're way better than us!'

Three hours flew by, and it was time to head to the clubhouse: time for pizza!! The Irish kids were so excited, because they were ordering from Roma's, which made the BEST pizza in Ireland, and possibly the world. Ali and his friends also seemed delighted. So far, so good; everyone seemed happy and no signs of homesickness, although Ireland must be very different from Palestine.

The children seemed to inhale the pizza; it disappeared that quickly. The mums had made brownies and assorted cakes. They, too, disappeared in the blink of an eye. After dinner, Liam's coach, Marty, stood up and made a speech. He welcomed the boys from Palestine and talked about the week ahead. They would be travelling to Dublin to meet the Irish president and to train and play with a semi-professional team. Roy Keane would be visiting them in Ballyduff to coach the Palestinian team during a nearby football blitz with some local teams. There was one non-football day, and they would spend that day at the cliffs in Donegal and the beach. They would have a movie night on the last night with whatever food the boys voted on. The Irish boys and girls were already yelling, 'Roma! Pizza!'

Marty laughed, 'As long as our visitors agree to have a repeat of this food again.' The visitors cheered their support for Roma's too. 'Well, in that case, I think it's only fair that we let our visitors decide which movie THEY would like to watch. I'll need to know by Wednesday. Just in case it's difficult to get the film. Film night will be Friday, our last night together. Here's to a fabulous week that will unite us in friendship for years to come. Us and our countries.' The boys approved by shouting enthusiastically and loudly. Marty was a great speaker and coach. He always made sure the team was inclusive and everyone had a fun time.

Back at the Murphys, Mary asked Liam to show Ali his room – their room – for the week. They would be sharing Liam's room. Ali started to laugh and said, 'No, there's been a mistake. I am not who I am.' The Murphys were all very confused, and the more Ali tried to explain, the more confused they became. Then Ali seemed to remember something. He went running to his bag. He brought a file to Gerry and handed it to him, as if that would explain everything.

Ali was quite adamant that he wanted to sleep in Sinead's room. It was getting late, and Gerry just looked at Mary and said, 'Look, they're all really exhausted. He's a good kid. Sure, Maisie even said so. Let him bunk with Sinead tonight, we'll figure it out tomorrow.'

Liam was disappointed and, if he was honest, also a bit hurt. He was hoping to chat more once the light went off. He really liked Ali and wanted to share things with him and get to know him better.

And Sinead? Well, she didn't know what to think, but she was flattered. One look at Liam's face, and she was even more pleased with herself. She showed Ali around her room. She quickly emptied a drawer for him, tossing all her clothes in a pile next to the dresser. Then, she walked to the closet and grabbed some clothes off their hangers letting them fall to the floor. 'You can use those hangers if you need them.' She probably didn't need to do that. Ali only had a small bag, but he smiled gratefully.

He noticed a doll on her shelf. Pointing to it, he commented, 'Such a beautiful doll, almost life-like.'

'Yes, isn't it? It used to scare me a little at night. I'd lie there watching it and couldn't sleep. Finally, I came up with a plan. I'd bring it into bed with me and pretend it was a friend. I always fell asleep then. It's really old. Like ancient,' said Sinead, stressing the 'ancient'. She continued, 'It belonged to my mother, when she was a little girl. And before that it belonged to my mother's mother, my granny. That was a really long time ago.'

She brought the doll down and placed it into Ali's lap. He was really enthralled by it and thought it must be great to have something that belonged to your grandparents.

Sinead said that she'd go to the bathroom to change. He could change in here, and she'd be back in a jiffy. Ali didn't know the word jiffy, but he got the meaning. He didn't know a lot of the words, but somehow, he managed. He understood about 60%. It was tiring, though, always trying to concentrate on what everyone was saying.

Sinead knocked on her way back from the bathroom. After hearing a quiet 'yes', she entered. Ali was on one of the twin beds dressed in a very feminine and very pink top with his hair down. His hair was lovely black, shiny, and down to his shoulders. Ali looked all of a sudden very girly. And pretty, thought Sinead.

Sinead just smiled. She was a little surprised but didn't want to be rude, so she hoped it didn't show. She was a very clued-in 12-year-old, so she knew all about non-binary kids. Or was it binary kids? She wasn't quite sure. One thing she was sure about was that he'd chosen **her** room . . . and her. She jumped up onto her bed and complimented him on his pj's. They **were** nice, and then she started in with 'How do you like Ireland?' That was the first of what seemed like a hundred questions to poor Ali, but he took it in his stride.

Ali seemed to fall asleep mid-answer to one of Sinead's never-ending questions. Sinead watched him for a while before falling asleep too.

Downstairs, Gerry and Mary were having another cup of tea. Gerry had put the paperwork from Ali's file onto the table. There were travel permits – quite a few – and lots of paperwork. And two passports. One was for Ali. The other was for a young girl with the same last name, maybe his sister. Gerry didn't think much of it; he just stuck it back in the file with everything else. And hoped 'the sister' didn't have her own travel plans this week! With no passport!

'It's all Greek to me! Or Arabic,' he laughed to Mary. 'They seem to be getting on great, don't they?' Without waiting for Mary to answer, he continued, 'It's great to see them communicating. You should have heard Danny trying to explain to one of them what a cliff was! Then he started to act it out, actually got on one of the tables – I thought he was going to fall off the table, but Marty interrupted his speech to get him down from that table. Ah, that Marty misses nothing.'

'Yeah, hopefully it continues to be as good as it has started,' laughed Mary at the thought of Danny standing on the table. The children seemed keen to learn about each other, their similarities and their differences. She was certain it would be a good week and they would learn so much about their different cultures.

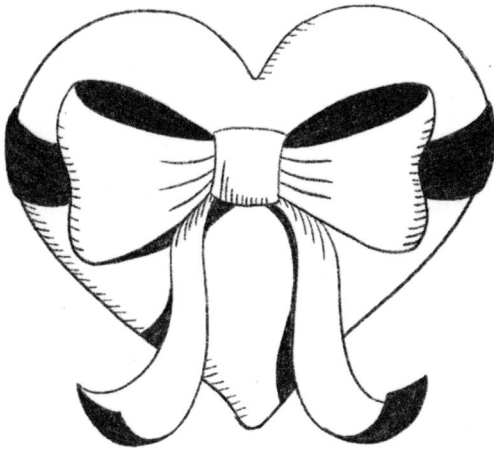

Chapter 3

Tears, Murder, and a Secret

The next morning at breakfast it was Liam's turn to ask

all the questions. What position do you play? Has your

team ever won their league? Who's your favourite premier league team?

'Liam', said Mary, 'Ali comes from Palestine. He probably doesn't follow the premier league.'

Liam ignored his mother and jumped up from the table, 'Come on, Ali, let's go practice penalty shots.'

The always-smiling Ali burst out crying and just stood there. He then excused himself, still crying, and hurried back to Sinead's room. Sinead looked questioningly at her parents and Liam, but they seemed equally confused. Sinead shrugged and followed Ali to her room.

She knocked, then pushed the door open a little to peek in. She could see Ali lying on the bed in tears. She didn't think about it and just walked in, climbed up next to him and hugged him.

In the kitchen, Liam asked his parents, 'What happened? I don't get it!'

Before they could answer, there was a knock on the door. Gerry went to open it and returned with one of the Palestinian managers.

Gerry made quick introductions. 'My wife, Mary, and my son, Liam. This is Saheed.'

Mary was on her feet immediately to make the obligatory 'cuppa'. 'Hello, you're very welcome. Oh, dear. You couldn't have come at a better time. Tell him, Gerry. I'm sorry – what did you say your name was again?'

'Please to meet you all. Saheed. I am Saheed. Is Ali here?'

'Yes, yes, there's just been a little problem. I'm sure it's a small misunderstanding,' started Gerry.

'Oh, Gerry, hush, what are you waffling on about? Ali is very, very upset. I'm not sure what triggered it, but he's run off to his room, crying. Can you understand? I'm not talking too fast, am I? Everyone says I talk too fast, so I wouldn't be surprised.'

'No, no, I understand. There's a slight problem with Ali. Can I speak to you both in private?' He looked at Liam, who could take the hint.

Feeling very dejected – first Ali, now this chap – Liam shouted, 'I'm away; ring me if Ali is looking for me.' This wasn't turning out at all like he thought it would. He went outside in a huff.

Saheed called him back. 'Liam, no, wait, I want to talk to you too. I just need ask your parents first something. Please wait. It'll only take minutes.'

Liam's spirits lifted a little, but he didn't show it and just nodded gruffly.

Liam stood under the kitchen window to wait. He wondered what 'the slight problem' with Ali was all about. He didn't have to wait too long. The window was ajar, and he could hear everything.

'I need to know I can trust you,' said Saheed gravely. Mary instantly looked worried, but Gerry was nodding his head, while saying, 'Of course, of course, anything you need, please just ask. You can trust us – all of us.'

'No, I don't want to trust anyone but you and your family. Can I trust your children? They are good kids, no? We asked around. We chose your family for Ali for many reasons.'

He looked earnestly at Gerry and Mary, who could see how nervous and tense he was. They wanted to reassure him, but words failed them, and they only nodded confirmation.

This seemed to suffice, because Saheed nodded too, 'Ali is no longer with us. He was killed.'

'KILLED!' shouted a startled Mary, who couldn't hold back. She stopped making the tea and sat down. She had no idea what this man was talking about. Ali was sitting in our Sinead's room was all Mary could think.

'Yes, there are many airstrike by the Israelis on our home, and many die. Many children. His mother – my sister – wanted Ali's sister to take his place. They were only year in age difference and very alike, in looking. Ali's sister is travelling as Ali, but for this week Ali's sister is Ali.' Saheed spoke very slowly, concentrating on every word.

Gerry and Mary said nothing. They just stared at him, waiting for more explanation.

'Do you understand?'

'Not really getting you there, Sameed, um, Saheed. Can you just say that again?' Gerry looked completely baffled.

'Ali who is staying with you this week is not Ali, but his sister. Ali is no longer with us. He was killed. His mother, my sister, wanted Ali's sister to travel,' he repeated even more slowly.

'What is her name?' asked Mary.

'I must be very careful. We will not use her name, so it hard for me to tell you without calling her by her name. We don't want you to know her name. It is just for, hmm, how you say, circumstances. Things could be very dangerous, if it was found out. We aren't sure we are doing right thing bringing her on this trip. My sister, though, is very adamant. She very hard to say no to. My sister happy she arrived safely here. We weren't going to tell you, but lay—' He stopped abruptly, gathered his thoughts, lifted his shoulders and continued, 'Ali's sister rang me early this morning. She said there was confusion over her sleeping in room of your daughter.'

'Oh, I see. Of course. That really wasn't a problem, in any case, but thank you for telling us. We will tell no one. The other boys on his team know, though?' Gerry said slowly, as if he wasn't quite sure what to think. Then he added, 'So Ali, sitting in our Sinead's room now, as we speak, is a girl? This boy – Ali you say – died, and his sister is here? And we are to call her by her dead brother's name?'

'Of course, she knows all boys on team well,' Saheed decided to concentrate on the first question. Then he explained, 'Her brother was good team player. Ali has

27

hamstring problem this week, and he will not play. He will still come to matches and be interested in them.'

'Liam, our son, his sister go to matches all, too. It be fine,' said Mary, who sounded like she was copying Saheed's accent, using some questionable grammar and speaking slowly like him. Gerry gave her a puzzled look. Under the kitchen window, Liam rolled his eyes and said to himself, 'Really, Ma?'

'I will respect your decision to tell your children or not, but I will stress that is against law, but with the system we live under, it could mean—' Saheed took a breath. 'Ali's sister could go to jail, be tortured in jail, lose residency of any country.'

'Why didn't she just travel on her own passport? You saw it, Gerry, didn't you? Wouldn't that have been easier?'

'Israel does not give travel permits easily. The team is very grateful for this trip. We've fighting to get this trip for years. First with a different group of boys and now this group. We weren't sure we would get here. Travel is very difficult for Palestinians. We need to get permission from Israel to leave Gaza. They don't grant permits for just anything – just sometimes necessary surgery, wedding of immediate family, **maybe** permits issued. But we have good people who helped us win our case. We wanted to do this for the children.'

'Oh, let's not tell them.' Mary was very quick to reply. She knew a little about Palestine but surely this man was exaggerating it all a bit. 'Let them just enjoy the summer. It's just a week. Let's not get too bogged down in the nitty gritty stuff.' Mary, herself, wasn't even sure what her thinking was. Her words were just a quick reaction. Maybe it was a mother's instinct to protect her children from stories of boys being killed, girls being tortured in prison, permission to travel being sought from Israel. How to explain all that to her children?

'I will – with your permission, of course – invite your son, Liam, to play with us. I will tell him he can take Ali's place. You see, Ali has hamstring problem.' He winked and smiled at this, which made them both laugh and helped to cut the immense tension that had built up in the room.

'Well, it would be up to him, but I'd say he'll be thrilled. Maybe if another lad could go along with him and, of course, he wasn't missing his own matches,' said Gerry.

Liam heard everything. He moved guiltily away from the window. He was smiling now. Oh, not because of some of the stuff, but the last bit sounded exciting. His team had nothing on this week except for a couple of friendlies with the Palestinian team, but he knew the Palestinian team were being feted and lauded this week. They'd been invited to play all sorts of teams. The president of Ireland, Michael D. Higgins, had invited them to his posh house for dinner, and Roy Keane – for God's sakes, Roy Keane – was going to coach them! He was so delighted, but then his thoughts turned quickly to the boy, Ali. He wondered what happened to him. Killed?! And so young. He wondered how that had happened;

why hadn't they heard about it? Surely the murder of a 13-year-old would be big news, worldwide.

When asked, Liam jumped at the opportunity to play right winger for Jabalia FC (Football Club). The extra player sorted, Saheed turned his attention to calling for Ali, who came running into his arms. She – no, he – was very glad to see her – no, his – uncle. This was going to get confusing. Ali. He.

Saheed held Ali tight and spoke Arabic to her. 'Everything will be all right now, Laila. You've only one job this week. Keep answering to Ali's name and enjoy yourself.' That's what everyone would have heard if they spoke Arabic, but they didn't understand, so they didn't hear him call his niece by her name, Laila.

The tea was finally poured for Saheed, much to Mary's relief. The kids went out to play and meet the other children. Training was at 11.30 am, so they had a couple of hours to play and explore. Saheed chatted to Gerry and

Mary. He was a lovely man with a beautiful big smile that pulled you into his universe.

'The trip was just an idea at first. But grew and grew. We've had Irish aid workers, who recommended to contact Marty, the boys' coach. He petition for this trip this end; we do same the other end. Finally, we get permission. To travel. Big relief. We planned to go through Israel, West Bank to Jordan and fly from Amman.'

'Would you not have just taken a flight from Tel Aviv?' asked Gerry, pleased that he had looked at a map of the area recently.

'Palestinians are not allowed to use the airport in Tel Aviv.'

'Really? Why's that?'

'Because we are Palestinians.'

Gerry shook his head, having trouble comprehending what he was hearing. 'Wow, I thought the days of outright racism were over. I thought it was a subtler game these days. That's a throwback. 'Back of the bus', if you're

Black or 'No need to apply', if you're Irish. Wow!' Gerry just shook his head in disbelief.

'**That** is quite shocking,' added Mary.

'Yes, there are many restrictions. Exit permits, entry permits – if you're travelling through Israel – then another exit permit, entry permit. It's a complicated process.'

'And what was the hiccup you encountered this week? It seemed like the whole trip might be off.' Mary nodded as if it all made perfect sense to her, but inside she was thinking, exit permits, entry permits, permission to travel?!

'Well, we had planned to go by Allenby Bridge. It is shorter route to airport in Jordan, near Amman, but very difficult because you must drive through Israel. Then West Bank to Jordan. There are many roadblocks and checkpoints. Surprise checkpoints too, yes? You could be held up for hours at one. Palestinians are only allowed to drive on certain roads, not good road. So, trip can take longer, very – how do you say? Unpredictable. We knew all this but had still planned to drive that way. But recently, Palestinians were being turned away. Soldiers tell them their paperwork is no good. Not true, but what can they do? Many miss their flights.'

There was silence for a while. Gerry concentrated on his tea. Mary pushed the plate of cakes towards Saheed. Gerry started to shake his head, mumbling, 'Well, I never….'

'Worst part is that you have only 24 hours to return to Gaza Strip when you enter back through West Bank. Via Erez Crossing. If you don't make it back within 24 hours, you will lose your ID and be treated as an illegal alien. On the way out of Gaza, you leave your ID with soldiers, so you need to pick it up again. It seemed too much to risk. We ended up driving to Egypt, then Jordan. We were not sure about permits to get out of Gaza by Rafah, but in the end, it was all good. We are here.' Saheed flashed a big smile.

Mary and Gerry smiled back, although they had questions. Many questions! Gerry was first with a question.

'Wow, that must be a bit further. My geography would have been useless, but I have been looking at the map – in anticipation of your arrival. Just out of interest, you know. We'd been reading up about Palestine too, but obviously we didn't read the right stuff. Yeah, wow, how much longer of a journey is that, then?'

'Maybe 8 or 9 hours extra. It's a lot longer, but safer. For us.'

Gerry nodded as if this was making total sense.

They concentrated on the tea again. Then Mary apologised, 'Oh, Saheed, where are our manners? I'm so sorry to hear about your nephew. So shocking. You did well to pick yourselves up and make this trip at all.'

'It was August last year.' Saheed nodded briefly with closed eyes but still managed to smile at them.

'Last August? And you couldn't get the paperwork for Ali's sister to travel in time as herself?' asked Mary.

'Oh, no, she would have been refused.'

Gerry slapped Saheed's back. 'Well, you're all here now. Let's make this a week for all of you to remember. If you've any problems, questions, you come looking for us. And don't worry about that wee girl of yours – I mean your nephew. We'll take good care of him.' He winked at Saheed.

They chatted a bit more; then it was time for Saheed to leave.

==========================

That second day was sunny and warm, a beautiful summer day. After training in the morning, they had lunch together; then they explored the area, with the Irish children acting as tour guides. Liam, Sinead and their friends were seeing boring Ballyduff through the eyes of the boys, and it made them appreciate what they had a little more. The woods didn't seem boring anymore. The Palestinians climbed the trees, jumped off branches. Their joy was infectious. The Irish kids had never had such a good time in the woods.

Ali and his friends took lots of photos. They said that their families back home wanted to see everything. Most Palestinians never leave Gaza. Danny was the best at pronouncing Gaza with an Arabic accent, but soon they were all saying it: Razza. The children laughed most of the day. Language barriers, different customs – they found it all hilarious. In the end, they had more similarities than differences. They were all children who just wanted to have fun and play.

They went back to their various homes for dinner, but then it was straight out again. They had spent the whole day outside. It had been brilliant. It was a perfect hot summer's day, and they were even able to swim and jump off the rocks at the lake until sunset which wasn't until around 9 pm. The Gazans were amazed how long it stayed bright.

'It is like 2 days in one,' Mohamad said. Mohamad was staying with Danny. He was also the captain of the Palestinian team and their star player.

The only one who hadn't been in the water was Ali. He explained that he had an injury, so had to be careful. He couldn't play football, but he was hoping to get back soon, so he wouldn't swim either.

Danny was suspicious. He noticed things and couldn't help wondering how swimming would so badly affect the hamstring, when climbing trees and jumping out of trees didn't seem to be a problem. He said nothing, though.

The second day was ending, but nobody wanted it to. They were quite happy sitting by the lake sharing stories and laughing. Around 9.30 am they heard the first parents calling their names. Soon more parents joined in calling names. The children didn't want the day to end, but it was inevitable. Day 2 was over.

Chapter 4

Second Night

That night Liam snuck into the girls' room. Well, technically, a his-and-her room. Liam wanted to tell someone. He **needed** to tell someone. All day, he had thought about telling Danny, but if Danny heard something was top-secret, you could be sure they'd know about it in Sligo the very next day. He thought about telling Sinead, but, yeah, she wouldn't believe him and would then go blabbing to Mam and Da. He even wanted to tell Ali. He thought it might help her/him to know someone knew his secret. Although he'd been bursting all day, he still hadn't told anyone. Ali was a girl! Secretly, Liam was glad.

The girls welcomed him. He squeezed onto Sinead's bed, but after a bit they pushed the two beds together. Tonight, it was Ali, who asked all the questions. She seemed particularly interested in Danny. Liam was thinking how typical; the girls were always interested in Danny – funny, good-looking Danny.

The three of them chatted for a long time: about the day, about movies, songs, food – even what they wanted to do in the future. Liam said that he wanted to be a footballer, even second division would suit him. Sinead wasn't sure. Ali said he wanted to be a doctor to help the wounded. Sinead corrected him, 'It's the sick, not wounded.' Ali shrugged but thought to himself, I think I'm correct. It is wounded in a war situation, which is what we have in Gaza all the time.

They tried to continue chatting and fighting sleep, but in the end sleep won. All three of them seemed to fall asleep simultaneously. They seemed to wake up simultaneously too, the following day. All three of them in the two beds pushed together. And just like that, the chat was off again. They were always talking. There was so much to share and learn about each other. Even Sinead and Liam seemed interested in each other, which was definitely not the case last week!

They had woken up early, which meant that they had a good hour to chat before breakfast. They couldn't believe that it was already Monday, day 3. The week was going by so quickly, and they were wishing that Ali was staying for two weeks.

'You'll have to come to Gaza to visit.'

'I'd love that, wouldn't you, Sinead?'

'Oh, yes, it sounds beautiful with the sea and the towns with the old buildings and alleyways. Let's work on Mam and Da, Liam. We should meet up next summer.'

'Yeah, and maybe you could come back with us for a week again?' asked Liam. He really couldn't imagine a world without seeing Ali every day. He might be falling for this boy.

'I would love that. Gaza **is** beautiful. You would love it, and you could meet my friends, like I've met yours.'

'Ah, sounds like you're getting a bit of a Ballyduff accent there, Ali.' Liam playfully tapped her shoulder. Ali smiled. She had the best smile.

'That's so true. You sound like a native!' Sinead agreed.

The chat was interrupted with a scratch at the door. Liam jumped up, and in came Maisie and Blacky. Maisie was crying.

'She has missed us. They usually sleep in one of our rooms.'

'But Mam said you might not approve, so they've had to sleep outside.'

'I'd love to have them as sleep friends.'

'Let's sneak them in tonight,' suggested Sinead.

'I'll sneak in with them tonight,' agreed Liam.

'Breakfast,' shouted Mary. They went running downstairs with the two dogs leading the way. Each thinking about the coming sleepover with the three of them and the two dogs in one big bed!

Chapter 5

First Match Day

The team had their first match on Monday. A neighbouring town's team was travelling to Ballyduff for a match at 7 pm. That meant no morning training. The team sheet was posted, and Saheed, good to his word, had put both Danny and Liam on the team sheet. The boys who were playing, the 'footballers', verged together. It was time to talk tactics and more. Mohamad told them that they should stay out of the sun to conserve their energy. That plan didn't last long! They ended up following everyone else to the lake.

It was a repeat of the previous day. Jumping and swimming and drying off in the sun. There were boats today too. Kayaks and rowboats. The craic – the Palestinians loved the Irish slang – was 90.

'Eat plenty!' Mohamad warned as they broke up for lunch. He wanted the boys to meet at 5 in the clubhouse for pre-match talks and warm-up. As their captain, Mohamad warned that there would be no time for dinner.

After lunch everyone raced back to the lake. It was just too hot for anything else. At least for the Irish. The Gazans thought it perfect weather – not too hot and not too cold.

Liam and Danny were drying off on a rock. Danny commented, 'Maybe they don't feel the heat, the way we do.'

'Yeah, probably not. It's proper hot in Gaza.'

'But then they've all been in the water except for Ali…' persisted Danny. He just let his sentence trail off.

'What are you trying to say? You know he has a bad leg.'

'Hmm, but he could walk into the water, just to cool down. That wouldn't hurt his leg too much. Hey, the cold water could be good for it. Maybe I'll tell him.' Then Danny shouted, 'Ali!'

Ali looked up and waved.

Danny waved back, just as Liam hit him. 'God, Danny, drop it. Maybe he doesn't want to go in the water. Maybe he hates the water. Maybe he's allergic to it. Actually, I think I heard something like that.'

'Really? He can't wash then? You always were a pathetic liar, Liam.'

'Well, I forget what it was, but there was some reason why he can't go in the water, so just leave it.'

'You'd think his best buddy would know that. Mohamad. He was telling me that Ali is his best friend in the world. He spoke past tense, but I put that down to his English. It's good, but he makes a few grammatical errors. Anyway, you'd think he'd know that about his **best** friend.'

'Well, I'm sure he does.'

'Then why did he just throw Ali fully clothed into the water? Ali obviously loves it. And look – he's actually a good swimmer too.'

Liam looked over. He couldn't help but smile. Ali looked delighted. And in no hurry to get out! 'Just drop it, Danny. They have their reasons. It's not for us to question why.'

'No, but I can wonder why **my** best friend was trying so hard to protect them, like there's more to this than he doesn't like water. You, Liam, have made me even more curious. A word of advice for you: don't get into the detective business.'

Liam and Danny watched as Mohamad had a towel waiting for Ali, who was now hurrying out of the water.

'So nice of Mohamad. Holding the towel for Ali. Maybe they're an item?'

'Maybe they are. So what?' Liam was not going to take the bait this time. He'd show Danny. He **could** be a detective, if he wanted. He didn't, but still.

Marty heard about Mohamad calling the players to the clubhouse for 5 … without dinner! He made a few phone calls, and the club house was decked out with banners wishing the boys good luck for their first match. There was also a table filled with sandwiches, vegetarian sausage rolls and drinks. Even Mohamad was glad to see the food. Playing all day had certainly made them ravenous.

The whole village came out to cheer on Gaza FC.

Liam and Danny slotted right in with the boys. They might look different, and talk differently, but football was a universal language. They understood each other completely on the field. Sligo FC were one of the best teams around. They were big rivals to Ballyduff, although Ballyduff hadn't beaten them in years, if ever. Really, it was no wonder. Sligo was a big town so could pick the best. Ballyduff played everyone – good or bad – and still only had 4 subs. It was always tight, and injuries were always a worry.

But Gaza FC dazzled. Mohamad was in his element. He led the team on the pitch. He was a natural leader.

It was 2-2 with the last two minutes of extra time. Liam was tackled in front of the goal and won a penalty. For his team – Gaza FC. (They had changed the name from Jabalia FC.) Everyone was cheering. Liam was delighted. Mohamad had scored both, and was the main striker, so Liam passed him the ball assuming he'd be the penalty taker.

Mohamad came over to Liam. 'Ali was our penalty taker. He was our best player. Today you play as Ali. You will honour us with the penalty.' Liam noticed the past tense. Danny was right. He made grammatical errors, but this wasn't. Unlike Danny, Liam knew the reason for it.

Liam coughed, 'Thanks, but that's not necessary. You take it. You'll win the game for us.'

Mohamad smiled, nodded and handed Liam the ball.

Liam was so nervous. Everyone was watching. He looked at the sidelines. Ali smiled at him. That big, beautiful smile. Her smile hit him deep, and he felt like his soul was lit up. He didn't want to let anyone down, especially not Ali.

He stepped up. He looked the keeper right in the eye, then in the top left corner and back at the keeper. He ran up, kicked the ball in the top right corner. The keeper had guessed the top left. The game was over. Gaza had beaten Sligo FC. The whole village erupted onto the pitch. They didn't care that it wasn't Ballyduff who had won. Sligo FC, their big rivals, had been beaten in Ballyduff.

Liam was buried by all his teammates. Everyone was laughing and hugging each other.

'Thanks, Mohamad,' Liam said after he crawled out of the tangle of bodies.

'No. Thank you. We've won our first match in Ireland. Thank you.'

It had been a great day. Liam and Danny had both slipped right into the team. They loved the Gazan boys, who treated them like minor celebrities, wanting to hear them talk and asking them questions. They learned a lot of new football skills from them too.

They learned other things as well. Sinead did too. They learned that life was complicated in Palestine. Growing up in Palestine was very different than in Ireland.

Chapter 6

Dublin Trip

That night Liam snuck into their room with both dogs. The dogs were delighted to be spending the night with the kids. They chatted a little about the match, but Blackie and Maisie were their focus for the night. Liam was in the middle of the girls with the dogs lying on top of him. Everyone was tired, and it wasn't long before they were all sleeping again. Liam was last to fall asleep. He waited until he was sure Ali was sleeping; then he reached under the sheets to hold her hand.

Mary called them early the next morning. Liam quickly let go of Ali's hand. They jumped out of bed. They knew today was the big trip to Dublin. Everyone was really excited. They were playing two Dublin teams and then going to Aras an Uachtarain in the Phoenix Park to visit the president of Ireland. Liam and Danny had been invited along too.

Mary told the kids that Phoenix Park was just like the country. So, it was decided that the dogs would join them. After the match, Mary and Sinead would walk them in Phoenix Park while the boys ate with the president, Michael D. Higgins, at Aras an Uachtarain. At least that was the plan, but plans can change.

Coach Marty and Mary drove behind the team bus with Ali and Sinead. Danny, of course, had to comment to Liam again. 'Ali is getting very close to your Sinead. He chose to sit in the car with her rather than the bus!' Liam was learning. He just ignored him and smiled. He wasn't going to give anything away. Also in the car were Blacky and Maisie! Of course. It was a big day for them too. Blacky and Maisie in the big city! That would be a new experience for the dogs. They were well used to watching football matches, but the city was another thing.

First stop was Crumlin United FC; the boys were playing the home team and a visiting team called Shamrock Rovers. They mostly slept on the bus, so they were fresh when they arrived. First teams to play were Crumlin United and Shamrock Rovers, while they watched on. News travelled fast that an ex-Irish National's son was playing. Robbie Keane Jr.! The Palestinians were impressed, and Danny and Liam were beyond amazed. Even more so when his famous dad came over to shake their hands and wish them all well. He was an Irish legend. He was really nice to the boys and posed for hundreds of photos! Even Ali, Sinead, Blacky and Maisie had their photo with him.

Next up was Crumlin United and Gaza FC. It ended up 2 nil with the home team winning. It had been a tougher match than the scoreline suggested. Next, they played Shamrock Rovers. They were defeated again. The boys were disappointed, but the coach from Shamrock Rovers came over to talk to Saheed.

He was really impressed with Mohamad's skills. He asked if he was playing regularly? Did he have an agent? Talk of agents was all new to the Gazan team, but Mohamad was delighted. Then Robbie Keane came over. He, too, had picked out Mohamad. He said he would keep an eye on him. He had just started managing a team in Israel, so he could invite Mohamad to visit and could go down to watch his matches in Gaza. He liked what he saw. Mohamad was so happy, but at the mention of

Israel, his eyes dropped. He nodded but seemed very disappointed. He didn't say anything, but he knew if Israel had anything to do with it, he would see no more of this Robbie Keane.

On the drive to Dublin, Sinead had said she, too, would love to meet the president. She wasn't asking or complaining; she only meant that she would have liked to meet him. Marty didn't think twice; he was immediately on the phone to his contact at Aras an Uachtarain, and, just like that, an extra place was set for Sinead.

The staff heard about Mary walking her dogs, so the president's dog walker joined her to show her the best places to walk dogs in Phoenix Park.

The house was palatial. The boys were enthralled by it and took many photos. They took photos in front of the house, inside the foyer, in the dining room, in every room! They wanted their friends and family back home to see the house. They were amazed. Finally, the main man himself came.

Michael D. Higgins met and shook hands with every player. He joked that Liam, Sinead and Danny looked very Irish. There were no airs about him at all. He was very approachable. One of his dogs joined them and was a big hit with the boys. He presented each Palestinian boy with a letter personally signed by him. He also had a plaque for their clubhouse back in Gaza that he presented to Saheed. He spoke about Palestine and their terrible living conditions and how important this trip was for the boys as well as their families back home. His hope was that it would give the boys and their families optimism and courage for the future. He talked about things happening in Palestine – bombings, land theft, fishing rights and unlawful imprisonments. He said that he hoped this would be the beginning of a long relationship between the two teams.

Every day, Liam, Sinead and Danny learned a bit more about life back in Palestine. They were devastated to hear, again, how hard it was for their new friends back in their homeland. Liam, especially, thought of Ali. He knew she'd lost a brother, and it made him so sorry for her.

However, it was a great night. There was a man playing the harp during the dinner. And the food was OUT. OF. THIS. WORLD! They had 5 courses! They were treated like VIPs (very important people), with waiters taking their plates with a small bow and asking if everything was to their wish. None of the children, Irish or Palestinian, had experienced anything like it before.

The president also congratulated Marty for working hard to make the trip possible and the Ballyduff FC team and their parents for being such gracious hosts to the boys. He presented Liam and Danny with a plaque for their clubhouse too. To say it was a good day was an understatement.

Finally, it was time to go. Everyone said their goodbyes to Michael and his dog, Misneach, and made their way towards the bus. Suddenly, Michael D. yelled out, 'Wait!'

Everyone stopped and turned around.

Michael D. Higgins knelt down to his beloved dog, 'What's that you're saying? Oh, do speak up, Misneach! I'm getting old and can't hear you!'

The boys were looking at the president of Ireland and then each other. Had this very important man lost his marbles completely? Liam didn't dare to look at Danny, because he knew that he'd make him laugh. Liam had gotten in trouble at school a couple of times by looking at Danny!

'Oh, yes, that's right! How could I forget?' The president looked up and called the boys back. 'Misneach just reminded me. There's a box in the hall, if one of you could go and get it. Misneach saved up his pocket money and bought you all a present too!'

Mohamad looked at Saheed, who nodded at him. Mohamad, a natural-born leader, stepped up and followed the president into the mansion. They returned shortly. Well, Michael D. and a box did! Mohamad was carrying an enormous box which hid him completely. Saheed ran to help him, but Mohamad insisted it was light.

'Go in peace, my friends. Open the box on the bus, and a safe journey back to Leitrim!'

Everyone hurried to the bus. They couldn't wait to see what it was. Sinead and Ali went on the bus, too. Saheed left his assistant coach, Fahmi, in charge and drove back with Mary and Marty in the car.

The box was well taped up. They were ready to give up, when Fahmi presented scissors from the first aid kit. Finally, the box was opened. Inside were the new Ireland FC shirts. Mohamad counted them. 18. That meant Danny, Liam and Sinead could have a shirt too. How did he know? There were 2 adult shirts, too, for Saheed and Fahmi. The boys were thrilled.

Nobody slept on the bus ride home. Everyone was too excited. They were going through photos and chatting about the day. Mohamad was especially excited. For the first time he dared to think of the future – something he didn't allow himself to do back at home – and it felt good. Once they'd gone through all the photos, Danny brought out his speaker. The boys (including Ali) and Sinead sang at the top of their lungs the whole way back to Ballyduff.

Mary, Saheed, and Marty had a quieter journey, although the dogs were snoring quite loudly in the back seat. Lucky Marty was sitting next to them. Saheed had a great sense of humour. Between him and Marty, they kept Mary entertained on the home journey and, crucially, awake. It had been a long day for Ballyduff FC's #1 fan.

It was late by the time they arrived back in Ballyduff. The boys seemed wired from all their singing, but it wasn't long until Liam, Sinead and Ali looked like they were sleepwalking. Mary, sensing that they were all very tired, just led them up to their rooms. She pushed Liam and the dogs in. Liam looked at her, surprised.

'You think I didn't know? You're a loud lot, the bunch of you, those two mongrels included!' she laughed.

Liam tried to stay awake to hold Ali's hand again, but he couldn't keep his eyes open. They all fell asleep without their usual chatter.

Chapter 7

Panic Sets In: Only 3 Days Left

Liam woke up in a panic on Wednesday morning. Only 3 days left! He really wanted to talk to Ali on his own. Her own. He wanted to tell her that he knew that she was a girl. He wanted to kiss her, if he was honest. Although he knew he couldn't do that; weren't Muslims very holy or devout or something? He didn't want to shock her. He wouldn't do anything like that. He just wanted to be her friend. A close friend. Honestly? He didn't know what he wanted. He was, however, panicking to think that Ali was leaving on Saturday. The girls were still sleeping, so he went downstairs.

'Hi, Mam.'

'Look at you! Aren't you up early this morning?'

'Yeah. I can't believe that they're leaving on Saturday. This week is flying by, isn't it?'

'Son, you get to my age, and every week flies by.'

'Do you think we should do something special for Ali?'

'Yeah, we could. What did you have in mind?'

'I don't know. Maybe one of your chocolate cakes with her name on it. Balloons?' He noticed that he had said her, but thankfully his mum didn't. It had been so hard knowing and saying nothing. Especially at home, when he tended to allow himself to think of Ali as a she.

'Yeah, that would be nice. Tonight or tomorrow? Friday is movie night and food at the club, so that rules Friday out.'

'Let's do tomorrow night?'

Mary agreed and suggested, 'What about asking Danny and that nice boy who is staying with him for a sleepover?'

'Yeah, I'd love to ask them **all**. They're all really nice, Mam.'

'Yeah, but we don't have room, and then it would have to be a cake for everyone, not just Ali.' She was thinking that she'd make two cakes: one for Ali and one for Mohamad. 'What about we do a sleepover at the clubhouse on the last night. I could talk to Marty. That might be fun. What do you think?'

'Yeah, I think they'd like that.'

'Okay, now get rid of your sad face. You want to enjoy these last few days. How about a cuppa before those sleepyheads wake up?'

It wasn't long before the 'sleepyheads' appeared. They ate breakfast and ran out to meet everyone. It was another beautiful summer day. Everyone kept saying that the visitors had brought the sun and warm weather. It wasn't long before most of the village kids had gathered at the field. Practice was at 11 am, and they had a friendly between the two teams later in the afternoon, so the boys mingled with everyone else. They walked to the shop and bought some crisps and snacks and walked to the river, where they sat with their feet dangling in the cool water. They always had so much to chat about. Today it was school, specifically, the similarities and the differences. School started for everyone at the beginning of September – only a week and a half away. The Gazans' approach to school was very different. They loved and felt privileged to go to school.

The Irish weren't so enthralled with school; it was just something that had to be done.

At 11 am, the boys went off to train. The coaches swapped teams to make it more interesting. Marty was coaching Gaza FC. Saheed and Fahmi were taking Ballyduff's team. Both sets of boys loved their new coaches.

In between the football sessions they ended up at the lake. It was so hot; everyone wanted to go swimming again. Today, they had swimming races. Then a diving competition with a judging panel. Sinead was on it. She gave Mohamad the top score, but it was deserved.

The competitions were all in good fun, although some kids were more competitive than others. Their friendships had really developed by now. They knew who they could or could not tease, who the funny ones were and who the ultra-competitive ones were. They all got on so well. Really well.

Liam felt like they were the glue that Ballyduff needed. They just gelled. This week everyone was so accepting of each other and their differences. He was learning so much from his new friends. They didn't take life so seriously, but, at the same time, they did. Liam couldn't really explain it. They all wanted to be doctors, lawyers, engineers or journalists, and they thought about those things. Yet, they were always joking, 'if we even live to be adults!' Liam and his friends didn't really think of the future. The Gazans appreciated and liked school much more than Liam and his friends seemed to, but at the same time they were happy with everything that life threw at them. Take yesterday – they'd lost all their matches, but they laughed about it. Liam's teammates had been known to cry when they lost! They always took their football so seriously. Maybe they had it all wrong? School was important. Football not so much? Liam shook his head to himself. He would agree to disagree on that with them. Football always trumped school. Every time!

After dinner it was time for the blitz. They split up into 6 teams of 5. Marty explained the rules. It was a mini-World Cup blitz. Mohamad's team called themselves Palestine. Liam followed suit and chose Ireland for his team. Danny rolled his eyes and declared his team to be Argentina, and he would be the Messi of the team! Everyone laughed. In the end, Palestine beat Argentina in the final.

Chapter 8

The Real Magic and Another Secret!

The week was flying by, and the children were having so much fun. Everyone was outdoors all day every day, and phones were largely forgotten. Even the visitors forgot that they wanted to capture everything on camera for their friends and family back home. Liam and Sinead couldn't remember a week like it in Ballyduff.

The **real** magic, though, happened at night in Sinead's room, when it was just the three of them and the dogs! Liam still snuck in even though his mam said she knew. He wasn't so sure about his da. The three would talk about everything. They always had so much to talk about, with lots of questions on all sides. As the week progressed, Ali did more and more talking.

Tonight was no different. They piled into the make-shift bed like every other night. Then, Ali announced: 'I have a secret.' Liam was pretty sure Ali would finally come clean about being the real Ali's sister.

'My mother told me just before I left. She wanted me to know before I travelled, just in case something happened to them. I'm going to have a little baby sister or brother.' Ali could not contain his excitement. His smile just got bigger and bigger. 'The baby will arrive in December. I can't wait.'

'Oh, how exciting! Do you want a baby brother or sister?' asked Sinead.

'Well, I'd like a brother, but my mother wants a girl.' Ali hesitated before continuing, 'She thinks her boys are – how do you say – unlucky.'

'Unlucky? In what way?' questioned Liam.

'I have three brothers. They are all killing.'

'What do they kill?' asked Sinead.

'No, my brothers are martyrs.'

'I know that word, but what does it mean again?' asked Sinead, much to Liam's relief. He wanted to know too.

'They were killed for being from Palestine.'

'Oh, my God. Good God. That is awful. What are you doing about it? Actually killed!' gasped Sinead.

'I'm so sorry, Ali. That's awful. Really awful,' said Liam. He had heard about one brother, but 3!

Ali didn't say anything right away. Sinead walked over to the shelf and picked up the doll. She handed it to Ali.

'I like to hold her when I'm sad. You take her for tonight.'

It was only a simple act of kindness, but Ali burst out crying. Funny, though, she was still smiling. She didn't want them to feel too badly. She didn't want to upset them too much. She hugged the doll close to her.

Liam couldn't help himself. He didn't want to ask, but he had to. 'How?'

Ali took a deep breath. He dried his tears and sat up.

'Years ago, when I was just a baby, there was a bombing. Israel bombs us most years. My family evacuated to the school to be safe. My mother was feeding me and feeling . . . I'm not sure of the word. She was feeling crowded, like she needed more air. She wanted to sit outside. My mother looked around at her family. My father wasn't with us. It was me in her lap, my brother who was

73

a year older, and my older brother who was about 4 at the time. He was playing with other children, so my mother left him. She asked one of the other mothers to keep an eye on him. That she was stepping outside. She walked outside, sat on bench to feed me. Ali sat next to us on the bench. My mother had a sweet to keep him happy. She was just thinking how peaceful it was, and next minute a bomb hit the school. My older brother died. Motaz. I don't remember him, and we have no photos, because our house was bombed too. But we were okay. We have much to be grateful for. Praise Allah.'

'That's awful. You poor thing.' A shocked Sinead tried to offer Ali some comfort.

'It really is awful. Life has been so tough for you.' Liam waited before adding, 'That's one. What about the others?' He asked ever so gently. He had recognised the name Ali during the story and looked over at Sinead, but she didn't seem to catch on that 'our' Ali had a brother with the same name! He remembered her uncle saying that Ali had a brother a year older.

'Yes, my other two brothers killed last year. It was the year anniversary at beginning of this month. Momen was 5, and Ali was 12. Ali was the little boy who was with me and mum when Motaz was killed.'

'Ali?' asked Sinead, recognising the name now.

'Yes, Ali. They were both killed by a bomb. A gift from Israel.' Ali smiled at her comment. 'Momen was looking forward to starting school. He was going to use my old school bag. That made him happy. He couldn't wait to go to school.' Ali didn't realise why Sinead had questioned it when she used the name Ali. She was so engrossed in telling her story and had forgotten that an explanation might be needed. She ignored Sinead's question.

Nobody said anything for a while. Then Ali continued, 'My auntie moved in with us to help us after Motaz. My mother could not cope with the loss of Motaz and trying to care for two young children. My auntie helped her. Finally, over the years, my mother got better. She had no more children, until she got better. Finally, after 6 years, Momen came to us. And two years later, we have Hind. Now it is just Hind and me, so I would like a boy. I didn't think my mother would have children again. It took so long after losing Motaz. I thought it might take her 10 years before she was ready this time. Auntie says she's stronger this time, though. So, my mother wants another girl. No boys. Do you think it could be true that boys are unlucky in our family? I miss my brothers so much, so would like boy. I feel badly for even admitting that, you know, against my mother's wishes, so don't tell anyone.'

They were quiet. Ali hugged the doll. Blacky and Maisie, sensing the children's mood, snuggled into their laps. Liam and Sinead had heard so many sad stories that week. This one really hit them hard. Three brothers killed! Ali's mother had more children dead than alive!

'I have one more secret.'

Sinead looked devastated. She couldn't bear to hear any more sad news.

'I told you Ali dead. I now realise, Sinead and Liam, you must wonder. I am Ali. My brother was Ali. So, I tell you. This is very important you don't tell any of the other children. My name is Laila. I am Ali's sister. Your parents know too.'

'Laila! Such a pretty name. I feel like you are my sister. I feel so close to you, Laila!' She looked at Liam, waiting for him to add something. Sinead was very accepting of this news! Liam wondered if she had guessed, or maybe Ali had already told her?

'Hi Laila! I guess we have to actually keep thinking of you as Ali, at least for now or else the secret is out.' He smiled awkwardly. He was glad the secret was out though.

That night, when they were falling asleep, Liam did not wait for Ali to fall asleep first. He squeezed her hand. She squeezed it back. He really was falling for Laila. He fell asleep with a smile on his face.

Chapter 9

Bundoran Blitz

Thursday morning was another sunny day. Breakfast was a hurried affair. Today was a blitz with 10 teams, including Ballyduff FC and Gaza FC. Marty had rented a bus, and the smaller team bus, which they'd taken to Dublin, was also going. Everyone in Ballyduff had bonded with the boys, so they wanted to spend the last couple of days with them. There were a few cars going as well. It was like a convoy from Ballyduff to Bundoran.

Mary was too busy to go. Liam was surprised. His mum was their #1 fan. Sinead and Ali went on the big bus with a few other children who weren't playing.

They arrived in Bundoran by 9.30 am. Originally, it had been planned that Roy Keane would coach Gaza FC today, but that had fallen through. The Ballyduffers were more disappointed than the Gazans. They would have loved to have met Roy. They were certain that Ballyduff would have become part of Ireland's football folklore. Alas, it was not meant to be.

The first match started at 10.30 am, so Marty parked the bus in an out-of-the-way parking lot near a park. The doors to the bus opened, and on came a man – but upon closer inspection, this was not just any man, but

Roy Keane. He had made it after all! Everyone was very excited. He warmed up with them in the adjoining park and gave them a team talk. He was unable to stay to watch them play, but he had come! They were buzzing! Roy also had a private word with Marty and Saheed about Mohamad, who impressed everyone with his skills. The next 4 hours were all about the football. Both teams did well. Ballyduff were fourth overall. Every player got a medal. Gaza were second overall, and they got a trophy as well as medals. The Palestinians were delighted. Mohamad was singled out again. A few coaches gave Saheed their numbers. They were hoping he was staying in Ireland. Sligo FC were the winners. The team looked suspiciously different and older than the team that had played Gaza FC on Monday.

Mohamad was delighted, but he didn't stay long to talk to the other coaches, who wanted to praise him. He was in a hurry to follow the others. The beach was nearby and it was a hot, hot day, so everyone wanted to go swimming. The Palestinians were really used to the water and the waves, but they hadn't seen waves this big. They were soon riding the waves or diving into them. Everyone except Ali. Mohamad and the other boys took turns keeping her company, as did Sinead and Liam, of course. So, it wasn't really noticed that Ali didn't go into the water. Danny, the sleuth, though, noticed.

The beach next to theirs was filled with surfers. There were surfers from all over the world. They watched the surfers and the waves. The waves were enormous. The Gazans could not believe that these were normal waves. They were saying things like tidal waves and tsunami after checking Google translations. When they were hungry or thirsty, they ran to the chip van.

The day flew by, and soon Marty was yelling for everyone to make their way back to the buses. Danny had his speaker again, so they sang the whole way home. Marty and Saheed rolled their eyes occasionally, but it was all in good fun. They were overjoyed the children were getting on so well.

Soon they were back in Ballyduff. Their #1 fan was there to meet them. Mary must have felt she missed out, because it was only a short walk back to the house. She hardly had to come and meet them. She waved over to Liam, Ali and Sinead but was still looking around. Finally, she found the person she was looking for.

She walked over to Danny, who was last to leave the bus, stereo still playing the tunes.

'Danny, I spoke with your mum. You and Mohamad are staying at ours tonight, if that's okay.'

'Yeah, that would be great. We'll just get a few clothes and will be there in half an hour. Does that work?' Danny was smiling ear to ear. He loved staying at Liam's.

'Yeah, see you then. Bye for now.'

Mary walked over to her gang, who were waiting for her. She told them that Mohamad and Danny were coming later.

'Oh, I forgot all about that! That's why you didn't come with us today!' exclaimed Liam.

Mary just smiled. Back at the house, it became clear that she had been busy, **very** busy! The house was decorated with balloons. Two banners: 'Our Friend Mohamad' and 'Our Friend Ali'. The dining table was set for 5 places. The house smelled delicious. Mary was roasting chicken, lamb, lots of vegetables and potatoes. For starters, she had salad, smoked salmon or soup with fresh wheaten bread.

Everyone was excited. The table looked great.

'What about you and Gerry?' asked Ali noticing that the table was only set for 5.

'He's still working. Sure, when he comes, we'll eat in the living room in front of the TV. You kids can enjoy a night on your own.'

'Mrs. Murphy, you outdid yourself this time. This looks fantastic.' That loud voice could only belong to one person. Danny had arrived. He had a little backpack and, of course, his speaker!

'Where's Mohamad?' asked Mary.

'He thought it impolite or something, on account of his never being here before. He's knocking on the door, hoping you'll invite him in.' Danny rolled his eyes, and everyone laughed.

Mary hit him playfully as she passed, rolling her eyes back at him.

Dinner went down a treat. Blacky and Maisie got plenty too. Gerry arrived home just after the starters, grabbed a couple of chairs from the kitchen and joined the kids. He wasn't going to miss out. He wanted to hear about the blitz, the surfers and everything.

Mary had made two cakes: one decorated for Mohamad and one for Ali. One was a carrot cake, and the other was a chocolate cake. Ali didn't want to cut 'his' cake. He thought the decorations looked too good to cut, but he was outnumbered. Both cakes were delicious. Lots of photos were taken and shared with family back in Gaza.

Later, they were all in Sinead's room. Mary had blown up 2 air mattresses. They were doubles so there was plenty of room.

'Love the glam jams, Ali!' joked Danny, but it didn't go down well. Liam gave him a dirty look, and Mohamad said, 'Not cool, Danny.' He hadn't meant it in a mean way, so was a bit taken aback. Danny wasn't a cruel kid. He liked to make jokes, play the music and make sure everyone was happy. But he also didn't linger too long on the bad things.

'Okay, maybe we should get some Palestinian tunes. What do you two suggest?' asked Danny, clearly moving on from his bad joke. It worked. Ali had many suggestions: Elyanna, Ziad Abdallah, Samer. They played a few. Ali and Mohamad sang along. Then a folk dance came on, and they both jumped up and started dancing. This led to an impromptu dance lesson alternating between traditional Irish dancing and Palestinian dabke.

They ended with their friend's cousin singing rap. He was going to be the next big thing. Word was that he would be moving to LA. Mohamad rapped along.

'He wrote that song two years ago,' said Ali, when the song finished.

'Wow, when he was 12! That's amazing. It's deep. Is it really that bad there? It sounds like a fecking nightmare,' exclaimed Danny.

Mohamad and Ali looked at each other. They were able to speak without saying anything. They agreed that they would talk a little.

'Well, everyone knows someone who dies. Most people will have someone in their immediate family die.'

'Or taken away. Kidnapped,' added Ali.

'My best friend died,' Mohamad said. They waited, because they thought he'd say more. When he didn't, Ali added, 'My best friend died too.'

'Oh, Ali. And your poor brothers too.' Sinead reached out to touch Ali's hand.

'My brother was Mohamad's best friend,' added Ali, nodding.

'And my sister was Le—' Mohamad hesitated before he continued, 'your best friend.'

Ali said something in Arabic. Mohamad nodded, then looked at Sinead. Aware that it might seem rude to be speaking Arabic, he explained, 'Laila tells me you know the secret.'

'I don't know any secrets,' said Danny.

Liam grabbed Danny in a friendly headlock, and they both wrestled together. Mohamad joined in. The secret was forgotten. For now.

There was a scratch at the door.

'We forgot the dogs. They've missed our party!' Ali jumped up to open the door. Both dogs jumped up on one of the beds. They pushed the two double mattresses together and all moved to the floor.

'I want to ask you something.' Mohamad looked serious.

'Ask me – those two don't know nothing!' said Danny.

'I think I will come back. One of the coaches has been onto Saheed, our coach. He offered me to stay. I said no. I will go home and discuss with my mother. My father is missing. I have older brother, but I think I would like to try to play. This coach has place to live and small allowance. Dublin. Play with Shamrock Rovers. He will get me contract.'

'That's great. You really deserve it,' said Danny.

'I think you should come here. Marty could take you on. You could live with us,' said Sinead.

'Excuse me. I think he'd live with me!' Danny acted put out.

'Do you think that I should try this chance for football? If I can even leave Gaza again. What do you think? Laila? What do you think?' Mohamad stared at Laila. Danny noticed the name. Danny was smart, quick-witted and observant. He thought to himself: Laila? This isn't Ali. This is a girl, Laila. Danny guessed correctly, but unsure, he blurted out, 'You're Laila! Not Ali. That's why you have zero interest in football. You're a girl. Why? Why are you pretending to be a boy? Do you want to be a boy? But you don't, do you? You're a girl and happy to be one. What is going on?'

Stunned, everyone forgot about Mohamad's question. Liam went first.

'It's a secret, Danny. You can't tell anyone. It's really important that you don't tell.'

'Who am I going to tell? You all seem to know already.'

'Your parents! The others!'

'Why would they even care? But why are you acting like a boy? Poorly, I might add.' He smiled at Ali. She laughed. Danny had that effect. Ali repeated the story that she told Liam and Sinead the previous night. She finished with, 'Everyone was against me coming on this trip, but my mother insisted. She said I might not ever get chance again, and it could open doors, give me chances in life. She was right.' Turning to Mohamad, she continued, 'You should stay now. You might not get the chance next year. You might not be able to get out of Gaza again. So much can happen in a year. You should stay. It will help your family, if you are successful.' She seemed so earnest.

Mohamad smiled. 'I can't **not** go back. You know that, Laila.'

Laila nodded.

'Why?' Liam always had to ask.

'My father is missing. Israeli take him away. My mother is not so strong. She has suffered many things herself. I have to talk to her, convince her. I think if I have teams helping this end, though, I can do this.' He was looking at Laila for confirmation.

'Yes,' she said, but all the fun that they were having just 10 minutes earlier had disappeared. Laila looked very sad. 'Maybe. I could talk to her.'

'Let's call now. I will call my brother's phone.' Mohamad was already ringing.

A sleepy voice answered in Arabic. Mohamad, always very polite, told his brother that he was with Irish friends. Could they speak English? His brother switched right away.

'What are you doing ringing me now? It's 1 am. I thought something was wrong. How are you?'

'Hello, Abdallah! It's Laila!'

'Hi, Ali, I recognize your voice, but yeah, if you want, you can call me Salma,' joked Abdallah. He was a quick thinker, especially for someone who had just woken up. 'Saheed keeps giving us updates. You're okay, Ali? Hamstring is still sore and still not playing football?'

'Shh, I can't talk about that.' Laila didn't want to tell him that her secret was out.

'Yes, probably right. Well, tell me news.'

Mohamad swiped his phone to change to video call. 'This is my new brother, Danny. My friend, Liam. And my friend, Sinead. And, of course, our Ali!' Mohamad introduced everyone. They chatted for a bit, and then it was time to go.

Laila started to speak Arabic to Mohamad. Always polite, he translated, 'Laila is happy to see someone from home. This is all she says.'

'Will you stay or come back next year? I thought you'd have asked your brother about the football offer,' said Danny.

'I try to come back next year. I can't stay. I have to make sure mother is okay with plan.'

Everyone could see how serious he was, and obviously things are very different in Palestine. So, he wasn't just ringing and talking to his mother or his brother about it. The whole thing left them with more questions than answers. Liam couldn't help thinking that Laila was right. There was an offer now; take it. He could sense it was not the right time or place to voice his concerns.

'You should come back too, Ali. Or Laila. Now I don't know what to call you.'

'Please call me Ali. Mohamad is stupid,' she smiled at Mohamad as she said this. 'He calls me Laila all week. They all do. No one noticed.' Everyone laughed. Eventually, most of them drifted off to sleep. Liam and Danny were still awake. Danny was very serious, for once.

'Liam, it is such an unfair world, isn't it? I mean, just think what they've been through. God, I can't imagine going through the half of it.'

'I know. It's awful, isn't it? They seem so brave about it. Like it doesn't affect them that much.'

'It affects them. There's so much pain in their eyes. Not all the time, but sometimes. All of the boys. I wonder what **their** stories are. It's like they all have had tragedies. And Laila?' He whistled.

'What's that meant to mean?' asked Liam, annoyed.

'She's a stunner – tell me you haven't noticed!' Danny could pick up on Liam's mood change. So, our Liam fancies the Palestinian girl, thought Danny. That's a pity. I'd fancy her myself.

He kept that to himself and just said, 'It's sad for her too. Her brother and her best friend dead.'

'Three of her brothers! Dead!'

'No way.'

Liam just nodded. They were quiet then. Both thinking. Eventually, they, too, drifted off to sleep. Liam's last thought was 'I wish I could hold your hand again tonight, Laila.'

Chapter 10

Last Day and Good-bye

They woke up early the next morning. Everyone was
excited. They were going to Slieve League in Donegal
for a hike along the cliffs, then for a quick trip to the

beach and finally back to the clubhouse for a massive sleepover and movie night: *Coco*. The Irish kids had recommended it, although it was meant to be the Gazans' choice! Marty suspected as much, but he went along with it.

It was another perfect sunny day. They had been blessed with the weather that week. The cliffs were stunning. Danny, Ali and Mohamad walked the One Man's Pass. Sinead and Liam went around it. The steep descents were making them a bit nervous. Of course, Danny had to pose and take photos on the Pass. They spent so long at the cliffs that there wasn't time for the beach. They waved at the beach as they passed. Danny was, of course, playing tunes, including the new Palestinian tunes. It was fun to watch the Gazans really rocking to their songs.

Everyone enjoyed the pizza and the movie. Plus, the parents had brought salads, chips, sausage rolls and a few cakes. Mohamad said that they were certainly well fed on the trip. It was the perfect last day of the week. After the movie, Danny became DJ extraordinaire. Mohamad, Danny, Sinead, Ali and Liam danced the *dabke*. Their practice the night before had paid off. Then, the Gazans got up and danced it. Danny, Sinead and Liam watched with everyone else. Their performance was powerful. Soon, everyone was jumping around to the music. There was a lot of chat too. They didn't drift off to sleep until 5 in the morning!

Marty had to wake them up on Saturday morning. The overwhelming feeling that morning was sorrow. The week was over, and nobody wanted it to end. Ali, Sinead and Liam walked back to their house. Once Ali finished packing, he came into the kitchen, where all the Murphys were waiting for him. He entered with his bag. He bowed his head and, holding back his emotions, said, 'Thank you for time here. I am very grateful. My mother was right to fight for this. There were many – how do you call it – discussions, but stronger than discussions about whether I should travel. I'm grateful to you, to everyone, my mother, the coaches, the boys on team, but especially you. You kept my secret all week. I would like to introduce myself. I am Laila.'

Sinead repeated, 'That's such a pretty name.' She thought this every time she heard Laila being pronounced in Arabic.

Ali/Laila nodded and continued, 'Ali would have loved this trip. I am very sad that he didn't get the chance. He would have liked all of you very much and you liked Ali very much.' Still fighting her emotions, she continued, 'I feel very positive after this trip, like anything is possible. It is so hard for us to travel, but we fight all the barriers, and we are here. Shukran, thank you.'

Liam, 'Will we call you Laila now?'

'For now, I am still Ali.' She smiled at him. Her smile always penetrated so deeply, like it could light up his soul. He was upset that he hadn't been able to hold her hand the last two nights. There had been too many people around. He really wanted to tell her how much he liked her, but feared he wouldn't get the chance.

Mary turned to wipe her eyes a little. They were all heading to the airport soon, but they had time for one more cuppa and some fresh cake that she had baked. She busied herself to keep the tears at bay. She had also made cakes and sandwiches for the team for their trip.

Sinead presented Ali with quite a big package that she had wrapped. 'For you, but don't open it until you're back home. You must promise.'

Ali smiled, 'Of course, of course. And thank you.'

Next, Liam presented her with a little gift. 'You can open my present on the plane.'

Gerry was next. 'From Mary and me. Ali, you are always welcome in our home. You are special to us. There will always be a little of you in our hearts. Come anytime and stay for as long as you wish. My kids haven't fought all week, so whatever influence you have on them, we greatly appreciate it,' he joked, as he handed over a package.

Mary was still struggling. 'Ali,' she said, choking back her tears, 'you can't know how much we loved having you here. And like Gerry said – all that.' She just pointed, waved her hand and nodded.

'You can open **our** present now,' said Gerry. 'I went to great lengths to pick it out.' Gerry laughed at his own joke.

Ali unwrapped the present. Inside was a new pair of trainers, a shirt, sweatshirt, hat and another small box wrapped. 'Oh, my, I can't accept this. It is too much.' Her smile was radiant, and she was holding up the top to have a closer look. 'It's all very lovely. You picked well, Gerry!'

'Open the box!' urged Sinead.

Ali opened the box. Inside was a delicate gold Celtic cross with a gold chain. Ali bowed her head and held her hands together. 'Thank you for your kindness. I will remember you always.'

Gerry, who wanted to avoid a crying fiasco, said, 'Right. One last cuppa for the road. And let's see what goodies you have to go with that?'

Ali gave the dogs a big hug. They looked dejected like they knew Ali was leaving for good. Then everyone climbed into the car. The trip to Dublin was uneventful. Everyone felt too sad to talk.

And the good-byes at the airport were practically unbearable. Thankfully, they were quick. Mary stressed that Ali's mother and family would be so glad to see her again, hoping to get Ali thinking forward and not over the past week.

Saheed and Fahmi gathered the whole team together, and they left for the departure gates. The Murphys and the other Ballyduff families watched them leave.

'That was an incredible week. They taught me so much. I think they left a mark on all of us,' said Marty. Everyone agreed, nodded and wiped away tears. Slowly, they all left, saying their good-byes with calls of 'See you back in Ballyduff.'

The journey home was even quieter. Downright gloomy. Sinead and Liam set up a WhatsApp group with the 4 Murphys and Ali in it. Then another one just with Ali and the 2 of them. And a third one with Danny and Mohamad added. Liam sent Ali a quick text, 'I miss you so much already. Heartbroken. Come back soon.' Almost immediately came a reply, '♥ ♥xx'. He really wished he had said something. It had been so hard with the whole Ali/Laila thing. He hearted her message and closed his damp eyes, causing a lone tear to escape.

On the way home, Sinead and Liam both fell asleep, but they woke up as the family was driving up their drive-way. Gerry got out of the car first and let the dogs out of the house. They came running to greet them but ran past them. The dogs were looking for Ali too.

Was it really only one week since they had all arrived?

Chapter 11

The last week before school

It rained on the Sunday after the Gazans left, and it was

cold. There was no swimming or much playing. Everyone

was walking around with their heads down. They were just waiting for news from the travellers.

They had texted Laila/Ali throughout Saturday. Everyone was relieved when, on Sunday, they finally had word that they had arrived safely back in Gaza. Laila/Ali had made it back home! Ali had opened Liam's present on the plane. Liam had printed out a few photos. There was one of Ali, Sinead and the President of Ireland. There was one of the three of them with Mohamad and Danny and one of all the Murphys including Blacky and Maisie. He had framed his favourite. He had taken out a photo of him and Sinead from a frame in his bedroom and had replaced it with a photo of just Ali and himself to give her. He hoped she liked this photo more than the others.

He got the text that he had been waiting for when Gaza FC had arrived back in Jordan. 'Liam, thank you so much for the photos. I will cherish them forever, especially the one of you and me, xx.' He didn't want to read too much into it. He knew now that Ali put xx at the end of all her texts in the group chats or to Sinead. Probably even Danny! He was, however, hopeful; she did say she would cherish their photo the most.

At the Murphys there was a lot of talk about next summer. Liam and Sinead were keen to travel to Gaza and bring back Laila for a visit. They had finally started to think of her as Laila. There had been a lot of texts back and forth, and once she arrived back in Gaza, she felt comfortable signing off with Laila.

'It's funny thinking of her as Laila,' said Gerry one day.

'Oh, no, she was never an Ali. Laila suits her much better,' said Sinead. Everyone laughed at her earnestness, and Liam privately agreed. Laila suited her.

Sinead had received a text from her after Laila had arrived back home and opened her present. 'Oh, my special Sinead. You are like the twin that I never had. Thank you so much for grandmother's doll. It has been in your family so long. I love it, but I will care it for the year. Until we meet next summer, then you must take it to carry on your family tradition and give it to your daughter. I am glad to have it, though. It makes me feel closer to you. I sleep with her every night. Please know I want you to know I take good care of your doll. Many thanks, your sister, Laila xx.' Then she added, 'I cried when I saw it. I know how much that doll means to you, Laila xx.'

Sinead didn't share that text with Liam who was always asking if she'd heard from Laila. That first week after Laila left, Liam even slept in Sinead's room. It seemed right, but slowly things returned to their old ways. Still, something was missing. Both Sinead and Liam felt it.

Chapter 12

School Starts

Soon, school started for both the Gazans and the Ballyduffers. There were fewer texts back and forth. Liam was busier with school, football and homework.

Sinead, too, was busier with camogie, school and home-work. They were both in grammar school now and had to take a bus to and from school. The coursework was harder too.

Laila and Mohamad had sent photos of their friends and their houses, but school slowed down the stream of messages from their end too. They did send a photo of their first day of school with Hind, who was 3, waving good-bye.

Even though there were fewer texts, they still felt involved in each other's lives. They had already shared so many photos of families and friends that Sinead and Liam felt they knew half of Gaza.

Danny said Mohamad had brought the football up with his mum, and she wanted him to do it. He hadn't even needed to convince her. Coach Marty was looking for the best club for him. Danny joked that he was going to be Mohamad's agent. He sent him information on the various clubs, so he could make 'an informed decision'!

Danny would put on his agent voice, when he explained all of this. It made them laugh.

There was plenty of talk about visiting Gaza and bringing Laila back for another holiday. Gaza looked beautiful. Danny had invited himself along for next year's Murphy Family summer holiday 2024. Everyone had fallen into a routine. They were happy – to a point – again. There was a lot to look forward to. Still, something felt incomplete.

The first month of school flew by. Soon, it was October. There was a lot of excitement because Coach Marty had found a good contract for Mohamad, and it got 'agent' Danny's stamp of approval. Derry FC, who had a great academy and were second in the league, had looked at the videos of Mohamad. They would organize accommodation, school, football and even a small stipend. Marty said that there would be premier league scouts at the matches too. Danny said it was better than Dublin, because it was only 2 hours away.

Everyone was super excited. It made the distance between them seem not so far. Mohamad would spend Christmas with Danny's family before his new adventure in Derry started. Derry FC was taking care of paperwork and visas. Everyone was excited. Mohamad would be here in just over 2 months!

Other than that, October was the same as September: school, after-school activities, homework, chores, food, sleep and repeat.

Then, one Saturday morning, Sinead and Liam came down the stairs for breakfast. Their parents were there. They had news. Something terrible had happened in Israel.

'They killed over a thousand people. They came out of Gaza to kill them. It's absolutely terrible. And entirely unprovoked.' Gerry finished off explaining what had happened. He was shaking his head.

'Not sure about the unprovoked part,' said Liam.

'Son, God forgive you. That's an awful thing to say,' said Mary.

'Why? It's the truth. Why is it awful to say? Laila told us about . . . so many things. Mohamad too.'

'Yeah, she had three brothers who were killed. Mohamad's sister was killed. And there was other stuff. So much tragedy – wasn't there, Liam?'

'She had **one** brother who was killed,' stated Mary firmly, 'but that doesn't warrant killing so many people, innocent people!'

Liam replied, 'Oh, so that's okay? Her brother was innocent too! And no, Mam, she had **three** brothers killed. Ali and Laila's younger brother were killed last year. She had another brother killed when she was a baby. Mohamad's father was arrested with no charge – he was doing nothing – and they haven't seen him in years. His sister was killed. And his cousin. OMG, I can't even remember all of it. I wanted to forget! But they lived through it, and they can't forget. You could see the pain on their faces, whenever we brought it up.' Liam finished by storming out of the kitchen and up the stairs. Then his bedroom door slammed. Gerry and Mary exchanged looks. Gerry was mad and made to follow him, but Mary said, 'Give him a bit of time. It must be hard to digest that their friends' families could be responsible for such atrocities.'

Sinead spoke up, quietly at first, but her voice got stronger as she spoke. She was not going to back down. 'Mohammad's cousin was a girl. She had injuries from a bomb. She was young. Maybe 9. I don't know – I forget. She needed treatment. They had to get permission to get treatment in Israel. Then, they needed to get passes to travel. It took too much time. Time that the little girl didn't have. Laila told me. The girl was younger than me, but she had to travel with a stranger. Her **own mother** was not allowed to travel with her. And she died in Israel away from her family. I can't imagine how hard that must have been for her and for her family. Mum, there were so many stories like this. Laila told us. She didn't talk about revenge or hatred. You know Laila. How can you think she'd approve of this? But it certainly wasn't UNPROVOKED, as you say. They've suffered. Israel seems to go on a killing mission every year. Laila was telling Mohamad to stay here. Begging him. A year is a long time. She was telling him, warning him, you don't know what will happen. Maybe you won't get out of Gaza next year. Imagine your life being that uncertain! They talk about what they want to do, but they joke – yes, joke – ah, that is if we live to be adults!' Sinead stopped talking and just looked at them. Then she looked at the table. 'I'm not really hungry. Can I go up to my room?' She turned and left, not waiting for her parents' response. Her head was down, and she looked dejected.

'She might have a point?' asked Mary, feeling very unsure of herself.

Nodding, Gerry agreed, 'When did she get so smart? I feel like our kids gave us a lesson.'

'I feel like they've grown up too fast. Maybe it wasn't a good idea to host those kids last summer? I didn't realise how much they had heard. It's like a bit of their childhood was robbed from them.'

'Everything happens for a reason. You can't protect them forever.'

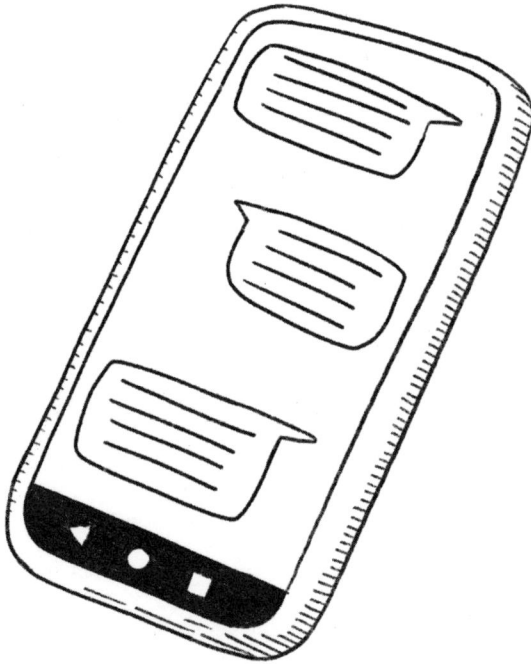

Chapter 13

The Aftermath

Liam was in his room, texting Laila and Mohamad. There was no answer. He texted the group chats: with Laila and Sinead, with Mohamad and Danny and with all of them. No answers. Then, finally, a reply. He grabbed his phone to check it. It was a message into the group chat with all 5 of them.

Danny: 'Hope you're both ok. Terrible what happened. Last year with your families.'

Almost immediately, Liam's phone rang. 'Hi, Danny.'

'Wow, it's crazy, isn't it?' asked Danny.

'What exactly?'

'I don't know. That Palestine and Gaza are in the news. You have heard, haven't you? It just seems so real since we know so many of them. Like, we wouldn't have even registered this 3 months ago.'

'Yeah, you're right. My parents are so annoying.'

'What did they say? It can't be worse than my parents! They said that a lot of them were terrorists.'

'Well, it **was** awful, what happened. Shocking. But it wasn't unprovoked – which is what my parents said. I mean, just between Mohamad and Laila, 4 family members killed and 1 in prison.'

'Do you think his dad did something? I mean, since he's in prison and all?'

'I don't know, but if I went through what Laila did, or if I were her dad . . . You know, losing 3 sons. God, how do you deal with that? And do nothing?'

'Yeah, I know. Well, I better go. See you later at the match.'

'Wait! What did you mean about sorry what happened to your families last year? In your message? In the group chat?'

'Ah, man, not even sure what I wrote. Let me check. Oh yeah, when I wrote "terrible what happened", I was actually talking about in Israel at that music festival, but then I thought that they're on the opposite side? Maybe? I don't know, so I added that about last year with your families. You know. I didn't want to piss them off, like.'

'Yeah, I get it. A bit random, but whatever. See you later.'

==========================

All the boys were super despondent at the match. Marty had to give an enormous pep talk to get anything out of the Ballyduff players. There was lots of talk about it all. None of them knew what to think. The biggest question was, 'Had anyone heard from any of the boys from Gaza?' Nobody had. They asked Marty if he'd heard from Saheed or Fahmi. Nobody hung around after the match. Everyone just drifted off.

There was a lot of talk about Hamas that week. Some reports said 1,400 had died at a music festival and a kibbutz and more were taken hostage. Liam, Sinead and Danny started a group chat. Everyone was downcast, and as news trickled in, their mood got worse.

Sinead: 'It's awful. All those dead babies. I think they were beheaded. Can you imagine? That's horrific.'

Danny: 'It is awful. 1,400 people killed. That's more than our whole village. Imagine all of us being wiped out?'

Liam: 'Yeah.'

Liam was very quiet – at school, at home and even in the chats. He mostly texted Laila, thought about Laila and looked at photos of Laila. He was worried about her. All of them. He had heard news of many deaths in northern Gaza, and that's where they lived. He spent most of his days worrying. Football didn't even interest him.

Danny was the most proactive of the group. He was reading everything, forming opinions. As the week progressed, he shared some of it with Sinead and Liam in their group chat.

Danny: 'Israel was handed to the Jews after World War 2. They just gave them a new country. But they took it from Palestine to give to the Jews! Israelis believe that they have a right to it, because years ago – and I'm talking back in the dark ages – years ago, they lived there.'

Sinead: 'Well, maybe it **is** their land, then? Israel's, since they used to own it?'

Liam thumbs-upped both comments. He was so numb. He couldn't get involved in conversations, but didn't want to seem rude, so hoped the thumbs-up emojis would suffice.

Danny: 'Na, Sinead, it's crazy stuff. There's a wall around Gaza. They can't leave. Israel controls everything going into Gaza. They can't even fish more than 10 miles off the coast. Israel cut off their electricity this week. It's mad stuff. Think of this: the Roman Empire back in the day included England. Can you imagine someone from Rome going to England, knocking on their door and saying you have to move out, because actually this house that you have been paying a mortgage on for the last 20 years belongs to my people because we lived here 2,000 years ago?'

Sinead: 'Danny! Let's keep to the facts.'

Danny: 'I'm telling you, it's true. I fact checked it and double fact checked it. Israel took over the Palestinians' land. Israel calls them settlements. They still do it. They just kick people out of their houses. Every year.'

Silence.

Then there were a few beeps on their phones. Danny had sent a few links.

Danny: 'If you don't believe me, read it for yourselves.'

Sinead and Liam started clicking on the links and reading. It **was** crazy stuff.

==========================

Sinead knocked on Liam's door and quietly entered. She climbed up next to Liam on his bed.

'I can't stop thinking about Laila and the others.'

'Hmm.'

'Did you read that stuff that Danny sent?'

'Yeah.'

'They live in a weird world. It seems so wrong. There's a wall around the whole of Gaza.'

Beep. Beep. Incoming message.

Danny: 'Apparently, no beheaded babies. Fewer people killed than said. Some were even killed by Israel's army. But check out some of these sites. Loads killed in Gaza and look at those buildings. Gone! Total destruction.' They were looking at some photos that he sent over.

Sinead gasped when she read that. Her first thought was that someone they knew had died. She'd seen a lot of photos of dead people in Gaza too.

Their phones beeped again. Another message from Danny. Liam turned his phone off without looking at it. Sinead was reading her phone, while admonishing Liam, 'Why did you do that? Rude!'

'Ah, Sinead, I've seen stuff. I can't look at it anymore.'

'What did you see?'

'Just stuff.'

'Tell me. Or I'll tell Mam.'

'It's all over insta, Sinead. Just look. Or read the news. Al Jazeera is good. Democracy Now is good.'

'What did you see, Liam?' Sinead was earnest now. She could tell Liam was serious.

'What did Danny text?' Liam asked to distract her.

'Something about people leaving their homes. Gazans.'

'Sinead, they've told everyone from North Gaza to leave their homes, but there's nowhere to go. It's not like they can leave Gaza. The Israelis are bombing everything. The photos—' Liam stopped talking. He didn't know how to describe the photos that he'd seen.

'I know that. Liam. I'm not stupid. I've seen stuff too. I know about how the Israeli minister said that they were all animals, and he was going to destroy everything. Block food, fuel, everything. And he would bring the place to rubble. I'm not stupid. You act so superior. You're only a year older, and that doesn't make you an awful lot wiser or smarter. I just thought we could talk about it.'

'Yeah, I'm sorry. I just wish they would text back. It's a week tomorrow, and we've heard nothing. I've seen so many photos of rubble. People leaving, but there's nowhere to go. People being killed as they try to leave. People looking for bodies in rubble. The whole of Gaza is so small, Sinead. It's only 25 by 6 miles. Or something like that.'

'I know. It's awful. It's awful on both sides. I do feel for the hostages, and the families of those who were killed.'

'The Israelis have already killed more Palestinians. In the first day. And the destruction. But yeah, I know what you mean.'

'It's awful. Does this make us terrorists by default? They say the Gazans are all terrorists.'

'Sinead, I don't believe a lot of what the media is telling us. President Biden said he saw photos of beheaded babies, but the White House said later that those photos don't exist.'

'Surely the President wouldn't lie?!'

'I think he wants a war. It makes money. Maybe there's oil? I don't know. I just wish one of them would contact us.' He looked at his phone, realized it was switched off, and turned it back on.

Beep. Beep. Incoming message on Liam's phone.

Sinead watched Liam as he picked it up. His face was transformed. He was smiling. Sinead realized it had been almost a week since she'd seen him smile.

'It's from Laila.'

Sinead picked up her phone. 'I didn't get a text?' Liam must text Laila privately. Well, she did too, so she should have guessed. 'What does she say?'

'We've been ordered to move, because of bomb to us. We moving to friend's house. My mother won't go to school. It has bad memories for her. That's where all my friends go. To shelter in school. I wish I go there. I might not text for a while, but we're all good. I'll text when I can. No wi-fi. No electricity.'

Sinead and Liam exchanged glances. They were so relieved. Liam wanted to run and tell his parents. Someone. Anyone. But it was already very late, so they texted Danny, who was delighted too. He still hadn't heard from anyone. Sinead fell asleep in Liam's room that night.

Chapter 14

One Week After

Liam woke first and went down the stairs. He stopped at the bottom step to listen to his parents. It sounded serious. His mum was saying that she was worried about 'the kids', especially Liam. He had been so withdrawn. And she wished that they had never had the children to visit.

'That was a great experience. I think everything happens for a reason. Maybe that reason will become clearer. Maybe we can help the ones who visited us. I'm sure it will end soon.'

'I hope you're right, Gerry. I'm thinking of ringing Karen McShane. You know, from college. She is a kids' counsellor now. She might have tips on how to handle this. They can see so much on their phones.'

'That's a good idea. I was talking to Marty. He was saying all the boys on the team are traumatised about it. Maybe she could talk to the whole team. Oh, Marty heard from Saheed. They're fine. He's sheltering with his family, Laila's family and Mohamad's family, so they're all good.'

'Oh. My. God. I can't believe you didn't start with that. Gerry Murphy! I'm going to kill you.' She started hitting him with the tea towel, but she was delighted.

'That's great news. About Saheed being in touch. Laila texted me too. She says that they're all fine.' Liam had a big smile as he entered the kitchen. His mum was so glad to see him smiling. She ran over and gave him a big hug.

Liam laughed. 'What's that for?'

'Just nice to see my son smiling again! Can't a mom hug her own son?' Mary was beaming.

'Ah, brilliant. And I'm sure it will all be over soon. What about the match today? Playing Harps at home?' asked Gerry.

'Yeah,' said Liam, and for the first time in a week, a week that seemed forever, he was looking forward to kicking a football again.

The day passed. They won their match. The Murphy family treated themselves to Roma pizza that evening. Nobody was checking their phones endlessly, looking for the latest updates on Gaza. It was a lovely day.

Lying in bed that night, Liam couldn't help but start to worry again. He had sent Laila so many texts, and her text didn't mention any of them. Not even hands praying on one of his texts. It wasn't like her. She always responded somehow. It made him worry again. Then he started looking at his socials. He had found a couple of journalists that he liked earlier in the week. Motaz. He searched that name, because it had been the name of Laila's brother who was killed. The first brother killed. The search led him to Motaz, a journalist, and he started following him. That led him to other journalists. What he saw was so graphic, so sad. It made him worry for his friends. He texted her again. Still no answer. Finally, he fell asleep, but it was a broken sleep.

Chapter 15

Third Week in October

Liam, Sinead and Danny checked their socials every day.

All of them followed Motaz now. Danny, who lived for

the next joke, had become very serious. Amazingly, he could recall so much information.

'Danny, I think you should go into politics. You're an encyclopaedia, when it comes to Gaza.'

Danny acknowledged the compliment with a quick smile, 'Remember how Laila and Mohamad used the word "aggression" for bombing? Strange word for it. I actually thought it was their English, or lack of it, but the media uses the same word: aggressions. It plays it down, doesn't it? Like, you get aggressive every time I nutmeg you, but you don't kill and bomb me.' Well, he could still make a joke, but a lot less than usual. And it might have been a joke, but the message was serious. None of them laughed. Danny continued, 'It's mad, you know. The media talks about Israelis who were slaughtered and Palestinians who died. Once you notice it, you can't help but see it everywhere.'

Liam said, 'That's why I stick with Al Jazeera or Motaz.' They talked about Motaz like he was a friend now.

The three of them were walking to the clubhouse. Mary's friend Karen was coming tonight to talk to the kids; then she was going to 'chat' with the parents afterwards.

'It doesn't look like it's going to end soon. I've asked Marty to try and get Mohamad over sooner. That would be at least one of them out. Marty thought it was a good idea. He shouldn't have gone home. He thought he'd have to convince his mum, but she was delighted and wanted him to come back here as soon as possible,' said Danny.

'If he'd mentioned it that night on the phone, he might have stayed,' said Sinead.

The clubhouse was packed. Karen waved over to Sinead and Liam. Then Marty started talking. It was a good evening. Karen explained that they should limit their time looking at social media. She told them that if they had any questions or saw anything disturbing, that they should talk to an adult or each other. She gave them her email and told them to get in touch if they felt unable to cope with something that they'd seen.

She didn't talk down to them. She explained that it would be better for them to do more proactive and constructive things than constantly looking at social media. She stressed that just because they were in Ballyduff did not mean that they could not make a difference. They could talk about Palestine to their friends at school, their teachers, their coaches. They could attend marches and fundraisers. An easy thing was to boycott stuff. They were all on board. The kids left the clubhouse pumped and ready for action.

On the way home, they felt energized and positive. They felt like they could be heard and could make a difference. They swore to never drink another Coke and never to eat another Big Mac. They all slept well that night. They were going to help their friends. They didn't feel so helpless.

After training on Thursday night, they made posters at the clubhouse. Free Palestine. Palestinian flags. They also learned a few chants. They were going to their first march on Saturday. There was no football match, so the whole team was going. It was in Dublin on 21st October, and Marty was taking the team bus.

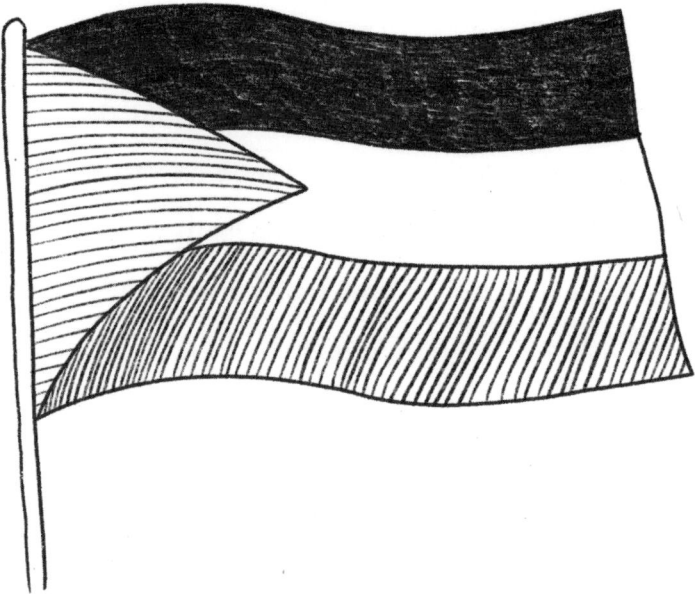

Chapter 16

Marching in Dublin

The day of the march had arrived. It was a good morning, but raincoats were brought. Just in case! There were a few extras from the village going, so the team bus was full.

Nobody knew what to expect. Was it a rally, a demonstration? Would the police be there? Would people be arrested? Mary went to ensure her kids' safety. They arrived in Dublin a little earlier than the 1pm start. Mary handed out lunches and drinks for everyone, and they ate in a grassy area close to where the bus parked. There was a hotel nearby, and Marty encouraged them to use the facilities. It would be a long day!

Soon it was time for the start of the march, so they walked the short distance to the Garden of Remembrance. The children were excited and proudly holding their newly painted posters. People smiled at them and nodded their appreciation at the posters. As they grew closer, they could see loads of Palestinian flags and they could hear singing and chanting. There were television cameras and stewards in hi-vis vests answering questions. The atmosphere was electric. So many people! All supporting Palestine!

'Wow, there are so many people. Let's take photos and videos. They'll love seeing this support.'

Everyone agreed that was a good idea. Soon they started walking. There was a girl nearby with a megaphone. She was chanting, and the crowd, including all the Ballyduffers, was chanting along with her. They walked down O'Connell Street, across the bridge, and in no time, they were walking around Merrion Square facing the Dail. There were speeches – lots of speeches! The children listened, but they were getting restless. The 'always prepared' Marty brought out a ball and took them into Merrion Square for a kick about. Mary and a couple of other adults watched on while still listening to the speeches.

Eventually, they made their way back to the bus, where more food awaited them – thanks to Mary. And hot chocolate! Mary had brought enough for everyone. There was plenty of talk on the way home; the children had lots to discuss. They were happy to see so many supporting

Palestine. It reinforced what they already believed: Israel had overstepped with their response. There had been a lot of talk about genocide. They, too, believed that it was a genocide, and from what they had heard from their friends, they believed this genocide had been happening for a while.

They sent photos and videos to their friends in Palestine, but no texts came back. Danny reminded them that there wasn't much wi-fi or electricity in Gaza, so nobody became too worried.

It was Liam and not Danny who asked, 'What about the tunes?' Danny was apologetic. He didn't think to bring his speaker! Nobody could remember a time when Danny had forgotten his trusty speaker.

Marty saved the day again. He had one. It wasn't as good as Danny's, but it did the job. They had a sing-along on the way home. Danny even played a couple of Palestinian tunes. When Marty's speaker died, they just started yelling the chants from the march. The bus arrived back around 9 pm. Everyone stumbled off the bus exhausted. It had been a long, but rewarding day.

Gerry had pizza from Roma's waiting on the table for his returning family. They ate quickly and retired to their rooms. Each lying in their own beds, Liam and Sinead contemplated the day. It had been a good day. Reassuring. Things would get better. They were sure of it. They both slept well.

The day after the march, Liam woke up to 4 texts from Laila! There were 2 messages from her in the group chats as well. Liam was so glad to see her name. This was the best day. He opened the first message.

'Thank you, Liam, for all your lovely messages. I am good. My family are good. But my parents fight much. Mother wants us to sleep together. We die together. She says is better. Nobody has to suffer losing family. My father disagrees. One might live to tell our story. Keep our family alive. They have agreed to alternate nights. One night we sleep together. One night I sleep with mother.

Hind sleeps with father. Then together. Then I sleep with father. Hind with mother. We are thankful. Allah is good. Laila xx'

Liam wasn't sure how to take this news. It sounded awful. It sounded scary. She was speaking of death like it might happen at any time. They all did, even in the summer when they were here. If we live long enough to become adults. They used to say that. He opened the next text.

'Liam. I didn't explain why I no reply. We have no connection. Saheed brings my phone with him to market, when he leaves to buy supplies. He goes to place for connection. That first message I wrote in hurry. I wrote on first day of this aggression. We had to leave home fast. I wanted to text you to let you know. Laila xx'

Liam opened the next message. 'I miss you. I bring not much from home. I brought photo of us, so I have close to me. Thank you. Laila xx'

And he opened the last message. 'I will write texts. You will only get when Saheed goes to connection. So, texts are old when you get. Please don't be sad. I am ok. You sound worried. I good. Allah will look after us. Laila xx'

There were two more from her. He opened the one from group chat with Mohamad, Sinead and Danny. 'Thank you for texts. I will show Mohamad. He lives with me. He phone not working, but I will tell Saheed to bring to connection. You might hear from him soon. Hope all are well. We miss you all. Laila xx'

Liam opened the last text from her. It was in the group chat with Sinead.

'Thank you for the kind thoughts and photos of Murphy home and dogs. Laila xx'

Liam was sorry when he had read the last one. He wanted more. He tried to reassure himself. She was okay. She had their photo. And this would surely end soon, even if Danny didn't think so. He went across the landing and knocked on Sinead's door. She was still sleeping.

'Sinead, wake up! Laila texted us. She's okay. Did you get any texts from her?'

Sinead rubbed her eyes. 'Oh, Liam, that's such a relief, isn't it? Let me check my phone.'

Liam waited, while she opened her phone. 'Oh my, yes, I've 3 messages. Two from our group chats. You probably saw those.'

Sinead read, "Sinead, I miss you and Liam very much. Please don't worry. I am good. Hi to Gerry, Mary, Blacky and Maisie. Laila xx.' Isn't that great, Liam? What did she say to you?'

Liam read out the last text to him about not getting texts until Saheed could get wi-fi.

Sinead read the other two messages. She had a big smile, as did Liam. Liam was happy to have heard from Laila but frustrated at the same time. He wanted more news. He sent a text to Laila. 'Maybe if you go with Saheed, we can text in real time or facetime?'

=========================

The children found it tough, but they were busy, and Karen's advice helped. They were planning a fundraiser at the clubhouse: Gig for Gaza. They met once a week to discuss actions that they could take. Marty said he was super proud of the team. Of course, the news coming from Gaza was awful. Every day seemed to bring something worse than the previous day, but they were trying to stay positive. Marty and Saheed were working on Mohamad; he didn't want to leave his mother. Derry FC were in touch with the foreign department to get Mohamad a visa. Marty contacted President Higgins to help speed up the process.

And, of course, they were hearing from Laila. Not every day. But a pattern was emerging. Saturdays seemed to be Saheed's day for the market, and late Saturday night he made it to the wi-fi point. All the messages would stream in then. Mohamad had given Saheed his phone too, so they heard from him. It wasn't ideal, but it was something.

Then towards the end of October, the messages started to come more often. They would get messages mid-week too. Saheed had found a place closer where they could charge phones and get a signal. The children were hopeful, but Liam often went to sleep with a wet pillow. He didn't think anyone should ever have to live through what he was seeing on his phone, and he was especially sad knowing his friends were living it.

They went to a march in Sligo the week after the Dublin march, which meant they were still able to play football in the morning. They had vigils in the village square mid-week. Every day they hoped for good news. Danny knew all the technical stuff like what kinds of bombs and fighter planes they were using. He also seemed to know more about Gaza's geography. He knew that most of their Gazan visitors lived in or near Jabalia. 'Don't you remember they called their team Jabalia FC at first, but then they simplified it to Gaza FC?' asked Danny. He decided that most of them lived in a refugee camp.

Danny was always studying and learning about Gaza. It was surprising because, before this, Danny lived for the good times and only the good times. But everyone had changed.

Danny and Liam were walking back from the school bus, and for once, Danny was positive. He had been looking up how many times Jabalia was bombed so far. They had been bombed on the 9th, 12th, 19th and 22nd of October already.

'No way! That's so much. I probably saw photos of some of those bombs. I don't really concentrate on the names of the cities. Are they still in Jabalia? Maybe they moved? Wasn't everyone told to leave?'

'Not sure. I'll have to ask Mohamad. But I'm taking a positive spin on this. If they've already been bombed 4 times, the IDF – basically that's the Israeli army, right? – has probably moved to another location. Some of those bombs are 2000 pounds. They wipe out whole blocks.'

'Not feeling your positivity there, Danny?'

'The IDF – actually I'm going to call them the IOF now – have moved somewhere else, and that means our friends have survived it!' Danny smiled, quite pleased with himself.

'Ah, you just said that you didn't know if they were even in that place. Most people probably left, since they were warned to, so maybe they have moved to a new place, and it will be bombed next.'

Danny took his phone out of his pocket. 'I'll just ask Mohamad now. 'Where are you? Where exactly in the Gaza strip?' There. Anyway, I think I'm right. They're safe.' Danny stopped abruptly; then he said, 'Oh, my dear God. This is bad. Liam, Jabalia has been bombed again. This time by 6 bombs that the US provided Israel. It looks bad. There are a lot of doctors, the UN and other agencies condemning this! God, I can't take much more of this. I wish we could just get them all out.'

'I said the same to Mam. She had actually looked into it. It costs 9,000 euros per person. Maybe we should use the money from the Gig for that?' They stopped, so they could look at the photos on Danny's phone. Liam was getting choked up.

'Ah, man, I've gotta go. That's just gut-wrenching stuff. I can't look. Hopefully, we get a text soon,' said Liam.

'Yeah, I'll take Karen's advice and switch off for a while.'

'Bye, Danny. A text from one of them can't come soon enough.' Both boys turned towards their respective homes. Both boys wiped at their eyes as they did.

Chapter 17

No News Is Good News

A week went by, and still no news from Gaza. Everyone tried to convince each other that no news was good news, but in reality, nobody bought into that theory. Mary had busied herself emailing TDs (members of the Irish parliament), signing petitions, starting petitions. Her car was filled with posters and flags, and she had bought *keffiyehs* – traditional Palestinian headscarves – for all of them. She was appalled by the images coming out of Gaza and determined to do her bit – and more. Dinners were a last-minute affair, but no one seemed to notice. Gerry, too, was affected and posting on his socials and attending the weekly vigils. He was planning on joining them at the next march in Dublin. It was a national march, and they were all going this time, even Blacky and Maisie. Sinead and Liam made the dogs Palestinian signs to hang around their necks. The activities kept them busy, but all anyone wanted was news from one of their friends in Gaza. The silence was worrying.

Finally, after a week and a half, Danny came by. He looked bad. Mary looked at him and told him to sit down. 'Ach, pet, sit there. You've news, haven't you? I'll just put on a cuppa; then you can tell us all. Liam, Gerry, Sinead!'

Mary called her family. Blacky and Maisie were the first on the scene; then the others followed.

'Well, spill it!' insisted Liam.

Danny took a big breath, 'I got a text from Mohamad. He's okay. Laila too.' Everyone breathed again. Danny continued, 'Laila's dad and Saheed are missing. They were getting supplies when it happened. They've disappeared. Mohamad and his brother searched the rubble, but can't find their bodies.'

'Oh, dear. That's awful. I feel so helpless,' said Mary.

'There's more. Laila's mom was really upset. She was pregnant. She had the baby 6 weeks early. She and the baby are okay, but in a different city. Forget name of hospital. Al Shifa, maybe. They are worried because hospitals have nothing, so they're worried about the baby and her mother.'

'Is it a boy or a girl?' asked Sinead.

'I don't even know,' answered Danny, feeling a little puzzled that Sinead's takeaway from everything was whether the baby was a boy or a girl?! Seriously, what was she thinking? Danny kept his thoughts to himself.

Mary pushed the tea to Danny and poured more for the others. Gerry tried to lift their spirits, 'We've the National March this Saturday, and next weekend is our fundraiser: The Gig for Gaza. I've been talking to our bank. We might be able to get a loan to get them here. I think that's what we must do.'

Mary looked at him, astonished. He had not said a word about talking to the bank. Gerry was always worried about debt. She smiled over at him. She agreed that they must do something. It must be why those children came to them last summer. Gerry had always said it happened for a reason. Well, this was it.

Liam put his head down on his arms on the table. He didn't say a word. He felt completely exhausted, drained, shattered. He couldn't hear the others talking. He couldn't even hear his thoughts, but he must have been thinking, because when he lifted his head, he said, 'At least they're alive.'

======================

Another week passed with no news. At this stage, they no longer tried to convince each other that no news was good news. They all knew better than that. The National March came and went. Blacky and Maisie were the major stars of the day and had their photos taken all day. They both lapped up the attention. Mary commented, 'They could get used to this city life. Look at them!'

It was good to be around people who felt the same. They all struggled, going about their daily tasks. School was unbearable. Mary was only able to concentrate on helping Gaza; Roma's was becoming a fixture at her dinner table. She had resorted to buying cakes for the obligatory cuppa. No homemade goodies could be found anymore in Mary's cupboard. Football was not the same, and Marty didn't bother with pep talks anymore. He looked in need of a pep talk himself. The only talk was about the gig this coming Friday night. And asking if there was any news out of Gaza.

But no texts came to them from Gaza. They saw photos of premature babies and wondered if one was Laila's little brother or sister. There were thirty-nine premature babies, but they had no oxygen, no incubators. They had to use polluted water mixed with formula.

The Gig for Gaza went really well. They made 9,000 euros. That was enough for one person or maybe 2 children to leave Gaza. Still no texts.

There was news that the premature babies were being transferred out of Gaza – thirty-one babies. Already, eight babies had died. They wondered, would Laila's sibling be with them? Still no texts.

========================

Finally, the news that they were all hoping for. A ceasefire. Surely this would be the end of it. First to hear the news was Marty. He had received a message: 'Please use this number from now on, 972 59 4567, I am looking forward to Ireland. Please arrange ASAP.' Marty was in the Murphy kitchen, discussing it. He was a bit wary, because it was so unlike Mohamad's usual messages, which he always signed with an emoji of hands praying.

Gerry said, 'Do you or Derry FC have the visa sorted? Just in case it is him. He was probably in a hurry. Text him. Maybe ask him something so you know it is Mohamad. But remember what they're going through is horrific, so if he isn't his usual cheery self, who can blame him.'

'Yes, visa is sorted, and Derry FC are paying for his passage. They also said it's only 4,500 euros for children. So, we can take 2 children in with the Gig's money. Possibly. Yeah, I'll text him on the new number.'

Not long after that, the tune 'Happy' by Pharrell Williams started playing. Everyone looked at Marty. They all knew Marty's ringtone. It suited him, normally, but not these past few weeks. His usually smiling face had turned glum.

'Thank you for texting. Abdallah writes this. Brother of Mohamad. Mohamad unhappy leave mother or me. mother wants him go. take chance. Please arrange me. We will get him to Rafah. He may take Saheed's orphans with him. We need sponsor for orphan. And money. We have 3,000 euros. Savings.' Marty read the message out loud.

'Maybe Laila could travel with him,' said Liam.

'Of course! She should,' agreed Mary.

'I've been onto the Department of Foreign Affairs about Mohamad,' said Marty. 'I've actually put all the boys' and Laila's names down for visas. Just in case. We've actually had to say we would sponsor them. I should add other names. Micheal Martin might be getting suspicious of that lad, Marty, from Ballyduff.' Marty giggled.

'Use our name. And other names too. He can get suspicious of Ballyduff as a whole, not just you.'

Beep. Beep. 'That's mine. I should get a ringtone like yours, Marty,' said Liam with a big smile. He could see the message was from Mohamad.   He walked to his room, as he read the text: 'Can you facetime? Laila x'. Liam didn't need to be asked twice. He phoned her back just as he plopped himself on his bed.

He could not believe it. He was looking at Laila. Beautiful Laila. She had the same smile. She was thinner, but she looked so happy. She filmed herself walking to her old house. The first time that she'd been back since 7th of October. It was bombed, but not too badly. She took him to a corner of her room and opened a metal box. 'Look, Liam. Sinead's doll. I put in metal box to protect. If anything happens, bring it to Laila. It will be here.' Laila's friend, who had been sheltering at a school, came unexpectedly. Liam watched as they hugged, cried, and hugged again. Mohamad was holding the phone. He waved to Liam while filming the girls' reunion. Liam was glad to see Laila looking so happy. Then Mohamad looked into camera, 'Liam, good to see you. It's been rough. But happy no more bombs. We can't find Saheed, and he had Laila's phone. We will share this one. I must go, battery low. But talk soon. Bye. Laila?' Laila's face appeared, 'Bye, my friend, Liam.'

And they were gone. Liam felt exhausted and shattered. He just lay on his bed. Sinead came charging in. 'What did Mohamad say?'

'It was both of them. Laila too. Her phone is gone, so she's using Mohamad's phone, if you're trying to get in touch with her.'

'Why didn't you tell me?' Sinead burst into tears.

'Sinead, they both said to say hello. She wanted to tell me where she put your doll, so it's safe for you, in case they don't make it. I didn't even realise you'd given it to her. Sinead, don't cry. She was thinking of you. That was the whole purpose of the call. She didn't want me to tell you that, but . . .'

'No, I'm glad you did. How did she look? And Mohamad?' Sinead wiped her tears away.

'They both looked great. Smiling. Really happy.' As he said it, Liam realised how surprised he was.

'Such a relief. You don't realise how pent up you are, but it's like I can finally breathe again.'

'Yeah, I feel that too. I think we dodged a bullet. There's a ceasefire, and they could both be here soon.'

Mary was in the kitchen, baking and cooking up a storm that evening. Mohamad and Laila texted quite a bit that day, like they had before October 7th. Electricity and wi-fi must have been restored. Everyone was so pleased about the ceasefire.

Mohamad and his brother travelled to Gaza City looking for Laila's mom and dad and Saheed. They didn't find any of them, nor did they hear any news of them. They did hear that the baby had been taken abroad for treatment. He was a boy, but Laila's mom wasn't allowed to travel with him.

Soon, Marty had visas for most of the team, so if ever they wanted to travel, the visas were in place. Gerry had secured a loan from the bank, if more money was needed for one of them. Others from Ballyduff were talking to their bank managers too. One neighbour joked, 'When we get all the boys back with their families, we can change the name to Ballyduff Gaza!'

The ceasefire was extended. Why didn't they just say it was permanent? Everyone knew there would be no more bombing. Liam, Danny and Sinead were glad to have their friends back. Laila videoed her sister Hind and Saheed's kids, her cousins, Amani, Dalia and Bayan. Amani, the middle child, was the same age as Hind. Laila helped to take care of them. Liam noticed these things. He was looking for clues about them all the time. They couldn't go back home. Jabalia and their home had been bombed again. They were living in a two-room tent. There was Mohamad, his brother Abdallah, his mother, Laila, her sister Hind, Saheed's wife and 3 kids. That made 2 adults and 7 kids. It was crowded. There didn't seem to be much of a kitchen. Food seemed in short supply, but his friends were always happy, even with Saheed, Mohamad's father and both of Laila's parents missing! 4 adults missing. But there were no more bombs. Liam was grateful for that.

They were careful not to mention football and coming to Derry. Mohamad's brother had asked them not to. He was working on convincing Mohamad. With the ceasefire, the Ballyduff kids were able to regain interest in football, camogie and, to a lesser extent, school.

Chapter 18

The Unbelievable Happens

The bombing started again. The ceasefire had ended!
THE CEASEFIRE HAD ENDED! Nobody could
believe it. Mohamad and Laila texted that they were

moving south. They could only bring what they could carry. Mohamad texted during the walk. He told them that people were shot walking beside them. They had been lucky – so far. They were headed for a place called Deir Al Balah. Laila said it would be lovely, because the beach was nearby.

They arrived tired and hungry. Laila refused to stay in the UN-based school. Her mother would not have wanted them to stay there. They ended up sleeping on the streets. Using Mohamad's phone, the usually happy Laila texted, 'I feeling happy to see the sea again. It usually looks so beautiful. I couldn't see the beauty. It didn't make me happy. First time the sea didn't lift my spirits. It's crowded here. Lots of litter. It smells. No bathrooms. Too many bombs and snipers. I'm scared. Again. Laila, xx'

Sinead and Liam were crushed. It was as bad as it had ever been. December began, and it was gloomy. Marty had no news about Mohamad's arrival. His brother, Abdallah, didn't text much. But maybe it was a good thing there was not much news from Gaza in Ballyduff. If there had been, it would have been grim reading:

Laila dreaded the nights. The nights were unbearably long. No one slept. Not even the children. They lay awake listening for the next explosion, guessing where it hit, judging how close it was. They all slept together. It did not make them feel safe, though. Laila could not remember what feeling safe felt like. The noise – it never stopped. Days were still noisy. Long lines for water. Long lines for food. Long lines for a toilet. Smoke everywhere. Rubble everywhere. Dust covered everything. Glass everywhere. The smell of smoke was preferable. The alternative was the smell of death. The smell of death must come from under the rubble. The noise. The noise. Never-ending noise. Laila was exhausted, sad. She didn't know how she could go on. She missed her father, her mother. She still missed her brothers. She missed Saheed. She was, however, thankful for Mohamad, his brother, his mother, her aunt and cousins. And somehow, she kept going, helping however she could. There was no news out of Gaza, so they didn't hear how bleak and harsh things were for Laila. They were spared that.

Liam wanted to ask Laila would she come back to get away from the war/genocide. But he resisted. And resisted. Until he could no longer resist. The answer he got was so disappointing, although Liam was expecting it:

'No, I could not leave Salma. Saheed's wife. Too hard with kids. We are all in this together. I have to find my mother. My father. Saheed. And my baby brother. And more than any of them, little Hind. I'm all she has from her family. I will never leave her. Laila, xx'.

The days dragged. And dragged. Finally, Abdallah texted Marty. 'Mohamad have papers. Laila knows. We haven't told Mohamad. He will take Hind and her cousin, Amani. Our thinking is to save the kids. They will arrive on Wednesday.'

Danny thought it funny. Funny strange, not ha-ha. Abdallah said that they would save the kids, but Mohamad and Laila were kids too. Kids grow up too fast in Gaza. He kept these thoughts to himself.

Wednesday? Today was Monday! There wasn't a lot of time. It was happening so quickly. Liam wanted to text Laila, but since she and Mohamad shared a phone, he resisted. He had an idea. He went to Coach Marty and asked to use his phone. He texted Mohamad's brother: 'This is Liam. This is for Laila. Is there any chance that you will change your mind and come?'

'Sorry, Liam, I can't,' came the reply immediately.

They had thought about taking the team bus to pick up Mohamad and the two girls, but it was decided that it was better not to overwhelm them. They were bound to be suffering from all the trauma that they had been living through. In the end, Marty and Gerry drove to Dublin Airport.

Waiting for their visitors in the arrivals hall, Marty couldn't help thinking about last August, when they had first met the boys. He was worried about this meeting. He was wondering what the toll of all the suffering would have on Mohamad and the two girls. Did those girls even speak English? He was tapping his foot nervously. Gerry put an arm out to him, and Marty managed to smile.

Eventually, the wait was over. There was Mohamad. He looked older, ashen, thin, but still smiling. And the girls? Marty scanned for the girls. Mohamad turned around to help someone, and as she came into view, it was not the girls, but Laila. She, too, looked older and thinner, but was smiling. Marty marvelled at their strength. How did they manage to smile so much? He kept looking for two younger girls, but Mohamad and Laila walked towards them. They didn't seem to be waiting for anyone else.

Gerry and Marty hugged the arrivals. Everyone was happy to see each other. Laila and Mohamad were looking around for others, just as Gerry and Marty had been looking for more travellers. Marty laughed. 'Sorry to disappoint you two. It's just us.'

'And it is just us. Hind and Amani did not travel.'

Marty was driving, and Gerry offered his seat to the travellers. Mohamad opted to sit up front. In the back seat, Gerry unpacked the basket that Mary had packed. He handed it out. They had an enjoyable trip home. They left the questions for another time. Marty talked about football in general, Ballyduff FC in particular and the weather. Gerry filled them in on Danny, Liam and Sinead.

When they were nearing Ballyduff, Mohamad explained, 'My brother planned this with you. I would not have come of my own free will. Laila, too, did not know she was coming until yesterday. We left my mother, Salma, Saheed's wife and the kids at our last camp. Laila and I travelled with my brother Abdallah. He had found Laila's mother and Saheed. Saheed injured in hospital, and his sister was minding him. She had been looking for him. Laila's father has been taken, but he is alive. We met with Laila's mother and Saheed. They wanted us to travel. It was too far for the kids. They speak no English. Laila's mother and Abdallah will go back to our tent. Saheed will be out of hospital soon. They know we are safe here and hope we can help them. We can work and send money. We can meet the others, if they come next. They insisted we come. It was hard to come, but parents know best. We are happy that everyone is well. Laila's father and my father are in prison, but okay. We are all okay. This will end soon. We can help from Ireland. Send money.'

Laila added, 'My mother said this was why she demanded last summer that I go in Ali's place. She has faith that it will work out. I will get job. Send money. She believes we can help better from here.'

Gerry and Marty just nodded.

It had been planned that Mohamad would spend the first night with the Murphys to get the young girls settled, so they drove to the Murphys. They hadn't even turned onto the Murphys' street, and the Murphys, their dogs and Danny were already out waiting for them – waiting for them on a cold, wet December day.

'Look, there's Mohamad sitting in the front,' said Danny. 'It only looks like two people in the back.'

Nobody answered. By now, the car was pulling into their drive, and everyone could see that there was only one person next to Gerry in the back seat. Gerry was hiding that person. For a split second, Liam thought it must be another of the footballers from last summer.

Gerry climbed out, revealing a happy Laila. Laila had come back! Mohamad and Laila were in Ireland! It was unbelievable! All three children were overjoyed. They went running to the car. Everyone was hugging everyone. When Mary found herself in Marty's arms, she started to hit him telling him to get away. Blacky and Maisie were barking and demanding hugs too.

Laila was the first to speak, 'How about a cuppa, Mary?'

'You bet, Laila. Follow me!' replied Mary, and she started humming a tune. Laila recognized it from the summer.

'Oh, I love that tune. You were always humming that! What do you call it?' Laila asked.

'Pennies from Heaven!' said Mary.

'Pennies and not bombs from heaven would be appreciated,' replied Mohamad.

Although it was incredibly sad what Mohamad said, everyone laughed. Mary put on a cuppa. 'I guess you'll be staying the night too, Danny?' They felt the future would be bright, even for Palestine. Little did they know.

END

Notes

_____

_____

_____

_____

_____

_____

_____

_____

_____

_____

_____

_____

_____

_____

_____

_____

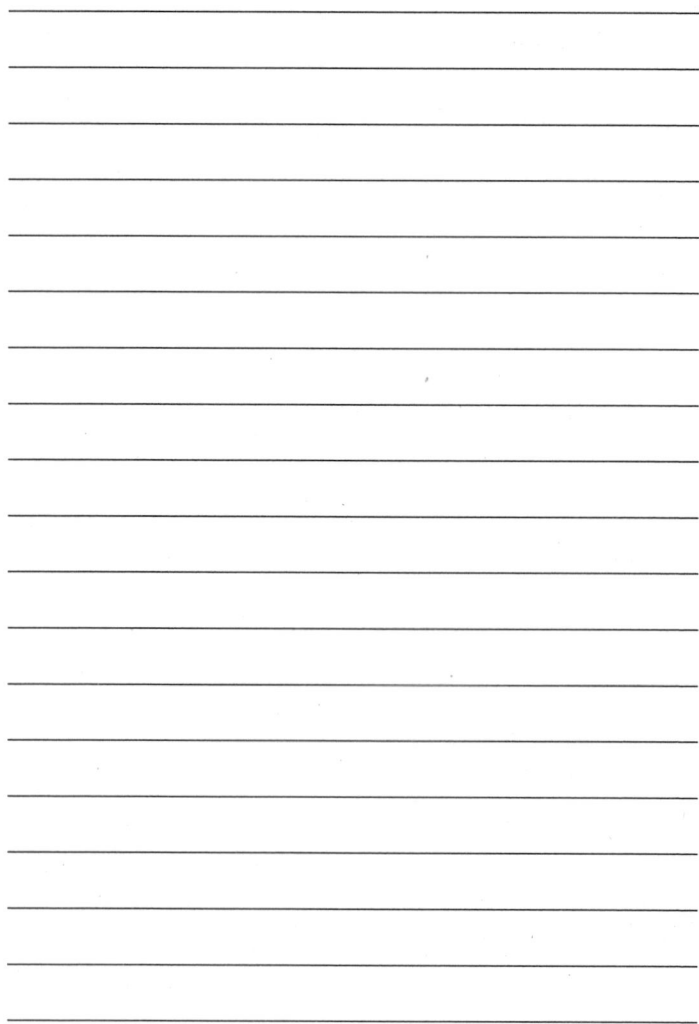